Praise for *Allie's Bayou Rescue,* Book One in the Princess in Camo Series

"*Allie's Bayou Rescue* is an awesome book to read together as mom and daughter! We love how real it was about the obstacles we face as girls—but not without a God who cares for us in our struggles, pursues us, and knows EXACTLY where we are going, AND HAS IT all under control—especially when we don't."

ELISABETH AND GRACE HASSELBECK, TV PERSONALITY AND DAUGHTER ... AND DAUGHTERS OF THE ONE TRUE KING!!

Running from Reality

Other Books in the Princess in Camo Series:

PRINCESS IN CAMO

Running from Reality

By Missy and Mia Robertson

With Jill Osborne

ZONDERkidz

ZONDERKIDZ

Running from Reality
Copyright © 2018 by Missy Robertson and Mia Robertson
Illustrations © 2018 by Mina Price

This title is also available as a Zondervan ebook.

Requests for information should be addressed to:
Zonderkidz, 3900 *Sparks Dr.* SE, *Grand Rapids, Michigan* 49546

ISBN 978-0-310-76250-8

Art direction: Kris Nelson
Interior design: Denise Froehlich

Printed in the United States of America

18 19 20 21 /LSC/ 10 9 8 7 6 5 4 3 2 1

To the entire Robertson Family: May we never forget the incredible opportunity God handed to each of us through a silly reality television show. And may we always remember the responsibility required in deflecting His light away from us and back to Him. "From everyone who has been given much, much will be demanded; and from the one who has been entrusted with much, much more will be asked," (Luke 12:48). I pray that what we as adults taught our children through this experience will help shape them into the next godly generation of Robertson world-changers.

—Missy

To Reed and Brighton: For always having my back when I need you the most; for being my older brother and sister and giving me a fun and safe place that I can always run to. I love you!

—Mia

Dear Person Who Is Reading This,

You have in your hands a top-secret journal entry written by Allie Kate Carroway.

Yes, I'm the Allie Carroway from the reality TV show *Carried Away with the Carroways.*

Yes, my family really is *that* crazy.

And yes, I *am* the girl with all the allergies. Why do people always want to know about that? It's not like I'm the first person to ever wheeze, sneeze, or have their throat swell up and choke them when they eat a peanut.

I'm sorry. That sounded a little . . . defensive. Let me start again.

You have in your hands a top-secret journal entry written by me, Allie Kate Carroway. I recorded it shortly after returning from a trip I took with my cousins to Los Angeles, California. It was the most magical week I've experienced in the twelve years I've been alive, and I *had* to write it down (and ask my cousin Lola to include a few sketches), since we have no video or photos to prove it happened. In fact, the whole thing was so unbelievable, I'm afraid I won't even believe it in a couple of years.

So, Person Who Is Reading This, I don't know how you found my journal, but you're one lucky duck. Get ready to be blown away, and encouraged—all at the same time—because that's what happened to me. But make me one promise: If you choose to read the entire story, you can't tell a soul what happened—especially my Papaw Ray.

Sincerely,
Allie Kate Carroway (Yes, *that one.*)

CHAPTER 1

9–1–1!

The day we filmed the Carroway Family Christmas episode—Friday, October 31st—was the day I ended up in the emergency room with a bunch of sick and injured trick-or-treaters.

The whole scene was weird. A huge, decorated Christmas tree, strung with multicolored lights, stood in the corner of my Aunt Kassie and Uncle Wayne's living room, and stockings—one for each person in our extended family—hung across their massive fireplace mantle. A bowl of Halloween candy sat on a tray by the front door, in case any of the little kids from the neighborhood came early to trick-or-treat. Christmas carols played on the sound system, and all my aunts, uncles, and cousins—dressed in ugly Christmas sweaters—took their assigned seats around three separate dinner tables and filled their mason jar mugs with sparkling cider for our traditional Christmas dinner toast.

It was taking forever for the film crew to set up, and I was starving. So, before I sat down, I snuck into the kitchen and grabbed a Rice Krispy treat from the dessert tray. I hid it in my pants pocket and listened as our director, Zeke, barked instructions.

"Okay, I know it's spooky and Halloween-y out there . . ." Zeke curled up his fingers to look like spider legs.

". . . but in here we're all merry and bright!" He smiled big and swung his arms around like a choir conductor. "Got it?"

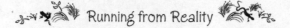

Most of us laughed, but Kendall, my thirteen-year-old cousin, sighed out loud.

"What-*ever.*"

"Hey—no grinches on the set!" Kendall's dad—my uncle Wayne—threw a napkin ball at her, and it smacked her right in the throat, which was covered by a leather choker. This one had a blue gemstone in the middle of it.

Kendall readjusted her choker and smoothed her straight, shoulder length, light-brown hair.

"Then can we really sing something? That would help me get in the spirit." Kendall loves to sing, and always looks for an opportunity. Lucky for us she's good.

"Not yet," Zeke said. "First we have to eat."

"I'm not hungry." One of my other preteen cousins, Lola, brushed her fingers through the pink streak in her short, dark-brown hair and grimaced at the green bean casserole in front of her. "It may look good, but we kind of know better, right?"

"But this is a new caterer, and I hear the food's delicious." Lola's younger sister, Ruby—who is the best baker I know besides my Mamaw Kat—poked a finger in the green bean goo, licked it, and then smiled.

"I'm willing to give eating a try." Hunter, Kendall's newly adopted twelve-year-old brother sat next to me and rubbed his belly. "I'm starving!" He reached for a roll, and right as he did, a freckled hand appeared from behind and knocked it down.

"Not yet, mister." It was Hannah, our wardrobe manager. Sometimes—okay, lots of times—her duties expand outside the boundaries of just controlling what we wear. She's petite, but she can be scary. And tonight, she had styled her short red bedhead to make her look like a zombie, and had drawn some zipper lips on her face with an eyeliner pencil.

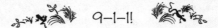

"Here." I broke off half my Krispy treat and discreetly handed it to Hunter under the table.

Hunter smiled, took the treat with one hand, and pushed his rectangular dark-rimmed glasses up on his nose with the other.

"Thanks," he whispered.

He started to lift the treat to his mouth, but stopped when Zeke began directing again.

"Okay, everyone. Here's how this is going down. Papaw Ray will give the toast. Then after you clink your glasses, Wayne will say a prayer. Then Kat'll serve the turkey, and y'all take it from there. Just have a good time, talk, and eat. When we're finished filming your table, we'll let you know."

"I can already tell this turkey isn't as moist as mine." Mamaw Kat used to make the food for all our episodes, but when the producers started scheduling several meal scenes a day, she couldn't keep up. That's when all the caterers in town began competing for the job of feeding the Carroways, and if I had to rank them, they'd all tie for last place.

"The turkey looks fine, Kat." My mom picked up a piece of turkey to inspect it, but then frowned and dropped it in the gravy boat. "There. Now it's moist."

Mamaw laughed. "Well, at least I'm cookin' our real Christmas dinner."

My stomach gurgled right then since my Krispy treat was not filling me up at all. I stood and faced the family. "People— let's get this thing done in one take. I want to hand out candy to the little monsters."

"Thank you, Allie," Zeke said. "Seems I need an assistant director with this bunch. Okay, when I say action, Ray, you're on."

Zeke yelled action, and the Carroway clan went to work filming "Christmas Dinner."

Papaw Ray began his speech as we held up our mugs:

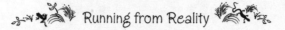

"Every year, we are grateful, and this year is no exception. God has allowed some challenges, but he has brought joyful blessings into our lives as well. This year, we are especially thankful for our new family member, Hunter. Every day is better with you here, young man. You've always been family, we just had to find each other."

"Here, here!" the grownups yelled, and they clinked mugs.

"Here, here," I said to Hunter, and we clinked. "Why do people say that during toasts?"

Hunter shrugged. "I guess because we're glad to be here?"

"Maybe because it rhymes with 'cheer,'" Ruby said.

"I think it's British," Kendall said.

"You want everything to be British," Lola said. Lately Kendall had been trying to speak with a British accent, like some of her favorite singing stars. The hilarious thing is that Kendall has the strongest Louisiana accent of all of us, so every time she spits out a British y'all, it makes me laugh.

"Would you bow your heads?" Uncle Wayne stared us down to quiet our table, and just as we were bowing, I noticed Hunter taking a bite of his Krispy bar.

I closed my eyes and tried to focus on thanking God for the food. This was being filmed, and even though I wasn't sure if I was thankful for this particular food, a prayer's a prayer—so I never pretend.

Uncle Wayne began:

"Father, we want to thank you for sending your Son to earth so many years ago . . ."

"PEANUT!!!!"

Hunter screaming that word right next to me made me jump and drop my Krispy bar on the floor.

"Hunter!" Aunt Kassie stood up and threw her napkin on her plate. "What is going on?"

14

Hunter opened his mouth and spit what remained of the chewed-up Krispy bar onto his plate. He pointed to the sludge and then stared at me with his wide, green eyes.

"Allie, the Krispy bars have peanuts in them! Somebody call 9–1–1!"

Now my mom and dad were up, and they swarmed me.

"A peanut? That's impossible! The caterers know Allie's allergic." Mom looked up at Hannah. "They know, right? All the other caterers knew."

Hannah pushed her way through to Hunter's plate to inspect the sludge. She sniffed it.

"I don't detect anything nutty."

I picked my part of the Krispy bar up from the floor.

"I haven't tasted any peanuts."

Dad bolted to the kitchen, and Mom grabbed the bar from me. She dissected it on my plate, pulling the yummy chocolate layer off the top. "It looks nut free to me."

Now Hunter was up and looking in every corner of the room.

"Allie, where's your emergency kit? You need to give yourself a shot!" He retrieved my pink wrist pack from a corner table near the sofa and ran it over. "Isn't someone going to call an ambulance?"

Dad yelled out from the kitchen. "Maggie!" A second later he stood in front of me. "I found a couple of nuts in each bar. Allie, did you taste a nut?"

"No, sir," I said, and I felt a knot form in my stomach.

Mom ran to her purse and pulled out her phone. "I'm calling 9–1–1. Allie, hit yourself with the needle, just in case."

Heat rushed to my face as I watched my family scurrying around. Lola, Ruby, and Kendall tried to push in close to me, but their parents pulled them away.

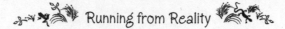

"Give her some space," I heard Aunt Kassie say, and then the cousins disappeared.

Exclamations of "Oh, no!" and "This is terrible!" echoed throughout the house while the cheery Christmas tunes continued to play.

"I'll go meet the ambulance," Papaw Ray said. "The rest of y'all better start prayin'."

Dad grabbed my elbow, lifted me up from my place at the dinner table, and led me over to the sofa. "How do you feel, Allie-girl? Is your throat itchy?"

I grabbed my throat and rubbed it. Was it itchy? Maybe. And maybe it was all in my head. I was certain I hadn't tasted any peanuts. But then, I hadn't eaten peanuts for years, so maybe I had forgotten what they tasted like.

Dad helped me fish the Epi-pen out of my medical kit, and he held my arm steady while I removed the cap and jabbed it into my thigh. The thing is on a spring-loader, so once you jab, there's no chickening out.

"Ow!"

I really hate that thing.

Mom came over with a blanket, and put it over me. "Just lay back and take it easy. Help is on the way."

"I really think I'm okay . . ."

"We're not taking *any* chances." Mom looked down at her watch. "Where is that ambulance?"

Dad stood up and placed his hands on Mom's shoulders. "Maggie, it's only been a couple of minutes."

Mom's hand flew to her forehead. "Did I forget to give them the gate code?"

"I heard you give them the code," I said. "Plus, they've been here a million times. I'm sure they have the code memorized."

What can I say? My family tries crazy things, so often

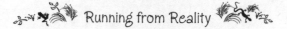

someone has to ride in an ambulance to the hospital. Sometimes it's a broken bone, or a cracked head. One time, my dad got bitten by a snake near the river, and his foot puffed up so much I thought his toes were going to pop off.

"I told you I should be doin' the cookin'." Mamaw brought a wet washcloth from the bathroom and laid it on my forehead. "Now don't you worry, sweet girl, you're gonna be just fine."

Hunter reappeared over the back of the sofa and nudged my shoulder. "Allie, hang in there. You have to be here for my very first Christmas as a Carroway."

"Hunter, I'm not going to die! I feel fine." I relaxed back on the sofa and focused on the tree with all the colored lights. Were they turning blurry? I shook my head a little, closed my eyes, and then opened them again.

It's just your imagination, Allie. Hunter may have eaten a peanut, but you didn't.

Or had I?

I tried to remember what it felt like the last time I did eat a peanut. It was at church, right after I was baptized, at our celebration reception. I thought the cookie was oatmeal, but no—it was peanut butter. I was so excited about all the events of the day that I just chomped away, not realizing I was poisoning myself. That led to a not fun couple of days in the hospital, and I promised myself I'd never do that again.

Apparently, I couldn't be trusted to keep a promise.

"Here comes the ambulance," Mom stood by the window and waved my uncle Josiah over. "Jo, can you go help Papaw direct them to the right door?"

"Sure, Maggie." Uncle Jo went to the door, and was greeted by little voices that said, "Trick or Treat!"

I turned and popped my head over the back of the sofa to see the first costumed kids of the night.

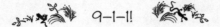

"Not fair," I yelled. "I wanted to hand out the candy."

Right behind the fairy princess and ogre came two para-medics, who rushed right over to me.

"Nice costumes," I said. "There's candy in a bowl by the door."

The first guy, a muscular one with short blonde hair, lifted my left eyelid and shined a light in it. "Allie Carroway, you're my favorite kid on TV." He flicked the light in my other eye. "Did you really eat a peanut or is that just a rumor?"

The second guy, also muscular, but with short dark hair, pushed his fingers into my wrist and then my neck. "Well, your heart's still beating—that's good for TV ratings." Then he smiled until his dimples caved in on both sides of his face.

Blonde Muscles spoke again, "Whad'ya say we get you out of here and make sure you live to see another season?" Then he grinned. It must be a requirement for paramedics to be charming.

"Can I ride with her?" Kendall was now at my side. "I sing, and I'm told that it calms people down."

"I don't see why not," Blondie said. "As long as one of her parents comes too. I think we can squeeze you in."

"How is she?" Mom came in from the side and placed her clammy hand on my forehead.

"She looks good. I don't see any sign of shock or agitation." Dark-Hair Dimple Man patted me on the shoulder. "But she's precious cargo, so we should take her in to have a once over."

"I'll call Dr. Snow," Mom said. "Maybe he can meet us at the emergency room."

"Should we all get in the cars and follow you?" Mamaw pulled a coat on over her bulky red sweater with the long-bearded Santa face on the front.

"Please," I clasped my hands and begged. "Can we just go ourselves in the car? This is embarrassing enough."

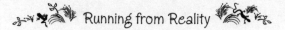

Kendall nudged me. "Oh, it's not embarrassing enough yet." Then she pointed over to the corner, where the film crew sat quietly with their cameras. Filming.

I could tell by the flickering red light.

CHAPTER 2

Can You Help Me?

The emergency room was packed. I guess others were missing out on giving candy to monsters too. Kendall took a seat next to me, and since it was now obvious I wasn't going to die, my parents disappeared into a side office to fill out some paperwork.

"I feel ridiculous wearing this." I was referring to my ugly sweater—red with gold candles all over it which was supposed to resemble wrapping paper on a Christmas present. The ridiculous part was the huge gold bow that felt like it stuck up a mile on my right shoulder.

"Mine's not much better." Kendall pointed to her blue sweater that had a Christmas tree on it. She grabbed one of the shiny pom-poms—that was supposed to be an ornament— and pulled it off.

She grinned, threw it up in the air, and caught it. "Wanna play catch?"

I shook my head. "Not feeling it right now, Kendall."

"Shall we see if the crowd would like to sing some Christmas carols?"

I looked at her with a straight face.

"That would be magical if it weren't *Halloween*."

"Can you help me?" A fairy princess with ultra-blonde curls who couldn't have been older than four approached me with a little plastic pumpkin hanging from her wrist. "I can't get this wrapper off 'cause my arm is a little bit broked." She handed me

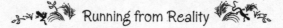

a swirly blue-and-green lollipop with her pumpkin hand. The other was tied up in a sling made from a camouflage T-shirt.

I smiled down at her and took the lollipop.

"Sure." I pulled the plastic off and handed it back to her. "How did you hurt your arm?"

"A ghost chased me. I ran away, but then I tripped on the sidewalk."

"Ouch," I said. "I'm sorry that happened." I looked a little closer at her sling, and noticed it was a *Carried Away with the Carroways* T-shirt. I almost told her who I was, but something stopped me.

"It's gonna be okay," the fairy princess said. "I got spongey bones. I been here before." She stuck the lollipop in the side of her mouth and kept talking. "Momma says I gotta stop runnin' all the time."

Then she turned and walked back to the corner of the room where some people sat who looked like her family members.

"Huh," I said to Kendall. "That was strange."

Kendall, who now had some earbuds in, pulled them out and turned toward me. "Did you say something?"

"Yeah. I said that was strange."

"What was?"

"That little fairy princess with the arm sling. She came all the way over here to me to ask me to help her open a sucker."

"What's strange about that? She probably recognized you from the TV show. Happens to me all the time. Plus, you've got that big bow that makes you stand out."

I shook my head.

"She didn't say anything about recognizing me."

Just then, a short nurse wearing a pink wig and a crown came through the electric double doors.

"Allie Carroway?"

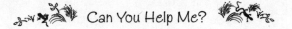

As soon as she said that, heads turned my way, and a buzz of conversation spread through the room.

"I wish she hadn't said that so loud," I whispered to Kendall.

I stood and walked toward the nurse. Kendall followed. Someone's phone flashed as they snapped a picture. Really, people? We're in the ER! I could feel all eyes on me—except two. The fairy princess was standing on her chair, the sucker stick still protruding from her mouth.

"Sit down, Emmy." A young woman dressed as a ladybug reached over and steadied the little girl. "Do you want to break your other arm too?"

Emmy giggled. "No, Momma."

Emmy sat down, and then she saw me. "Momma, there's the girl with the sprinkly eyes."

Emmy waved her sucker at me, and I waved back. Her mom laughed.

"You mean sparkly. She has sparkly eyes."

"Oh, yeah. Sparkly." She ran over to me. "Thank you. I knew you would help me."

I knelt next to her and straightened her T-shirt sling. "You're welcome. I'll be praying for your arm."

"Thank you. Can you pray I stop runnin'? I hate breakin' bones."

I smiled. "Sure. I'll do that."

"I knew it." Then she returned to her mom.

A funny sensation ran through my body as I followed the nurse to the exam room. Like tingles, but good. Or maybe it was peanut poisoning.

"Kendall, do my eyes look sparkly to you?" I turned to my cousin and opened them wide.

"Um . . . hardly. The white part is all bloodshot. And remind me again, what color are your pupils normally?"

"They're a rich azure blue! You know that."

"O . . . kay. Whatever you say. They're lookin' a little were-wolf blue right now."

We followed the nurse through a maze of white curtains.

"I'm sorry we don't have a private room for you, Miss Carroway, but it's been busy in here. Must be the full moon." She finally stopped and pulled one of the curtains back to reveal a bed and a little chair next to it. "Climb on up and we'll get your blood pressure."

I jumped up on the bed and Kendall sat down on the chair. The nurse grabbed a light stick and shined it in both of my eyes. Kendall tilted her head up and gave a little howl.

"Where are your parents?" the nurse asked.

I shrugged. "They went into some room with all my papers, and never came back."

"Maybe they were eaten by werewolves," Kendall said.

The nurse laughed. "Could be. There's never a dull moment around here." She pushed up my bulky sweater sleeve, strapped a band around my arm, and then pumped the little bulb and waited for the blood pressure machine to register some numbers. "Well, so far, so good." She stepped back and wrote some things on the papers attached to a clipboard. "It says here you may have ingested a peanut, and you're highly allergic." She pulled a tongue depressor out of a glass container and motioned for me to open my mouth. I did, and she placed the dry, wooden stick on the back of my tongue.

"Sounds like you got a trick and not a treat," she said.

"You have no idea," I tried to say, but it sounded more like "OO AHH OH EYE EEE UH."

"Hmmm. Things don't look swollen. That's a good sign." She referred to the clipboard. "Doctor wants some blood."

24

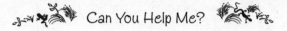

"Is he a vampire?" Kendall was having way too much fun for this being the emergency room.

"Could be," the nurse said, and she wiggled her eyebrows up and down. "Now that I think about it, the lab has been extra busy tonight too."

We followed her down a long hallway, where at least twenty people sat in chairs against the off-white walls, waiting to have their blood drawn.

"I'm going to go find your parents. Have a seat, and if you start feeling funny, alert the guy at the desk, okay?"

She pointed to a young, bored-looking twenty-something who was checking people into the lab.

"She hasn't laughed at any of my jokes yet," Kendall said, "So I doubt she's gonna feel funny, but I'll keep an eye on her." Kendall winked, and we both sat down.

Kendall watched as the nurse disappeared around the corner. Then she turned and gave me an intense stare. "Looks like it's gonna be awhile, so let's dispense with all the Halloween humor and talk." She crossed her arms in front of her and slumped down a little. "I've got some issues."

"Issues? With me?"

"No. Not with you. But with everything else in my life, and the number one thing on my list is the show."

"The TV show?"

"Yeah. I've been thinkin' lately that I need a break."

"A break?"

"Yeah. I'm just not feelin' it these days."

"Kendall, it's reality TV. You just have to act like yourself. What's not to feel?"

"Allie, don't you get tired of livin' your life in front of a camera? It's like we can't do anything without people knowin' about it."

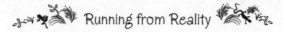

"Not true," I said. "Look at all the fun we're having right now without a film crew."

"Yeah, but all those people in the waitin' room were starin' at us, and takin' our picture. And you just came from having an allergy meltdown in front of the film crew. You know they're gonna want to use that footage for some kind of public service announcement."

"They will not. Mom and Dad won't allow it."

Kendall pointed a finger at me.

"You just wait and see. I know what I'm talkin' about. But hey, I'm glad you took all the camera attention away from me and my enormous zit."

Kendall then pointed to her chin, which did have a big blemish hiding under gobs of makeup that Hannah had used on her before our Christmas dinner filming.

I tried not to laugh, but it didn't work.

"Okay, so I look like a werewolf and you look like a goblin. Seems perfect for Halloween, right?"

"Yeah, but we were filming Christmas! Allie—that's another problem. Reality TV is confusing me! Look at what we're wearing." She reached over and flicked my bow.

Okay, maybe she had a point.

"Allie, don't you ever feel like we're livin' in a different reality than everyone else? I mean, what season is it really?"

"Well, I know in a couple of weeks it's going to be duck-hunting season."

Kendall jumped out of her chair and grabbed the sides of her head with both hands.

"No! Didn't we just have that?"

"Twelve months ago, yeah."

In the middle of November, most families begin to over-schedule and stress out because the holidays are coming. The

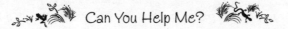

Carroways do that too, but we also add duck-hunting season, which means our dads are gone all the time. It's like throwing a battery into an already roaring campfire.

Kendall sat back down and dug her fingers into my arm.

"I'm not ready! I'm gonna get more zits, and I know I can't keep up with my homework, the filming, and all the extra chores!"

I pulled her hand off my arm and set it on her leg, so she could dig into her own skin.

"Kendall, aren't you the one who's supposed to be calming *me* down right now? Killer Peanut Sludge could be forming in my system to stop my heart as we speak."

Kendall turned to face me. "I'm so sorry, Allie. I don't know what got into me. Are you feelin' okay?"

She leaned forward to look in my eyes again and frowned.

"Still bloodshot?" I asked.

Kendall stuck out her lower lip and nodded. "They look worse."

"Great." I put my hands to my cheeks. "Maybe I do need a break."

"Excuse me, young lady. Can you help me?"

An older woman, wearing a purple sweat suit and using a walker with purple tennis balls shoved on the ends, shuffled right up to me. I sat up straight, and looked her in the eyes. They were clear and azure blue.

"I do believe I'm lost. I just stepped around the corner to use the ladies room, and now I can't find my way back to my husband. He's in the emergency department."

"Sure, I'll be glad to help." I turned to Kendall. "Save my seat, and I'll be back to the vampire line in a minute."

I stood and then walked slowly next to the woman.

"Hospital hallways all look the same to me," she said.

I nodded. "I know what you mean. They should paint the

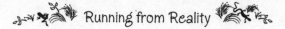

hallways different colors or something. Luckily, I just came from emergency, and I have a good sense of direction."

The woman grinned, and as we rounded the corner, her face lit up.

"Oh, there's my Howard!" The woman let go of her walker and reached out to give me a gentle hug. "I knew you were the right person to ask for help."

Out of all the people sitting in that long hallway? Weird.

"What's your name, honey?"

"Um, it's Allie. Allie Carroway."

I expected the name to ring a bell, but no.

The woman put her cool, fragile hand on my arm.

"Bless you, Miss Allie."

I smiled. "You too, ma'am."

"Thank you."

She grabbed her walker and started to move forward, but then turned back.

"Oh, where are my manners? I didn't ask you why you're here. Are you sick?"

I shook my head. "No. Just a little allergy scare."

"Well, I hope everything turns out alright."

"It will. I think I just need a little rest."

"Well, whatever you do, Allie Carroway, don't ever stop shining your light."

"Yes, ma'am."

I turned to make my way back to Kendall. The whole time, I wondered, *What light?*

CHAPTER 3

SOLD

The peanut scare turned out to be a dud—thankfully. But I was still bummed-out, because except for little Emmy with the fragile bones, I never got to hand out any Halloween candy.

"Dad, when exactly does duck-hunting season start this year?"

It was ten o'clock, and Dad was driving Mom and me home from the hospital. I sat in the back seat of our SUV, tired, and trying to come up with a plan to take a break from the upcoming "Deck the Halls and Ducks" madness.

Mom threw her head back on the cushioned headrest.

"Allie, why did you have to bring *that* up now?"

Dad glanced at me in the rearview and smiled. "Because she's a Carroway, that's why!" He turned to Mom. "She can feel the duck mojo in the air! I'm glad you asked, because the excitement all begins November 4th."

"That's too early!" Mom dropped her face in her hands.

Dad reached out and rubbed Mom's shoulder. "It's *never* too early! I'm gettin' goosebumps just thinkin' about it. It's the most wonderful time of the year."

"I thought that was supposed to be Christmas," I said.

Dad turned the car into our driveway, and as the garage door opened, his phone buzzed.

He looked at his screen. "Bayou's Best Realty. I wonder why they're callin' so late?"

He pulled into the garage, parked, and then put the phone on speaker.

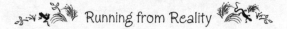

"Hello, this is Jake."

A high-pitched, rattly voice filled the inside of the car.

"Jake! This is Ellen. I'm glad you're still up. I have wonderful news."

Ellen is the lady who is trying to sell our house. After I added a mold allergy—complete with regular asthma attacks—to my medical resume, my parents decided to build a new allergen-free home around the block from our current house where I've lived for my entire life. It's supposed to take eight months to build it, if the rain goes easy on us this winter.

Ellen continued.

"You're not going to believe this, but I received an offer on your house today."

I unhooked my seatbelt and scooted to the edge of my seat.

"Really?" Mom laughed a little. "How so? No one's looked at the place all week."

"I know, and it's the strangest thing," Ellen said. "The family lives in Florida, but they sent the offer through their realtor over the phone. The gentleman said that he saw the house on the website and he wants to buy it, sight unseen."

"Are we talking about the same messed-up house?" I joked. Mom reached back and put her hand over my mouth.

"Oh, hi, Miss Allie," Ellen said. "You are such a funny girl! Yes, he wants your messed-up house, and get this, Jake and Maggie—he offered more than your asking price! AND . . . he's paying cash."

Mom gasped.

"Ellen, are you serious?" Dad poked the phone, taking it off speaker. I moved my head closer to try to hear, but Dad turned the volume down too.

"Mom, what does that mean, he wants to pay cash? Don't people always use cash to buy things?"

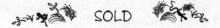

"Not for houses. Most people need to get loans from a bank for that amount. But if this guy has cash, and we decide to sell, it's pretty much a done deal."

A squirt of adrenaline made its way from my heart to my head and caused it to throb at both my temples. I pushed in with my fingers and closed my eyes a minute, trying to absorb what this all meant. I watched Dad's every move as he continued to talk to Ellen on the phone.

"Uh-huh, I see," he said, and he leaned his head back against the headrest. "And what's the catch? This seems way too easy."

He waited. And Mom and I waited and watched Dad's face. Soon a reaction came.

"Thirty days? That's smack-dab in the middle of duck season."

"What does that mean—thirty days?" I pushed Mom in the shoulder. "Well, what does it mean?"

"Shhh, Allie, I'm trying to hear." Mom leaned her head over near Dad's. He pulled the phone away from his ear and put it back on speaker.

Ellen rattled on.

"They need to move in quick because the man is starting a new job in your town. Do you think you can swing it? It's the most solid offer you're going to get this time of year, Jake. Wait, what am I saying? It may be the best offer you'll ever get."

Mom opened the passenger-side door and flew out of there, into the house. I waited to hear Ellen's last few words.

"I know it's sooner than you planned to move out, but hey—this could make a great episode for the TV show!"

I rolled my eyes and slumped back in my seat.

"It's right in the middle of duck-hunting season," Dad said, like he was in a trance.

"We've got forty-eight hours to respond with a counteroffer.

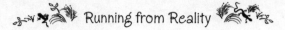

You and Maggie take some time to think about it and let me know."

"Duck. Hunting. Season."

Ellen laughed.

"You Carroways crack me up. Or, should I say 'quack' me up? Ha! Happy Halloween, Jake."

Ellen hung up, and Dad dropped the phone onto his lap. He sat there, frozen.

I climbed from the second seat into the front and grabbed Dad's cheeks between my two hands.

"Dad! Are you okay? We don't have to move in thirty days, do we?"

He stared ahead and talked in a monotone.

"I suppose we could live in one of the bigger duck blinds."

"Dad! What are you saying to me right now?"

Dad grabbed his beard and clenched his teeth.

"Allie-girl, hold on to your camo hat, because I think we just sold our house."

CHAPTER 4

Pack or Puke?

"Mom? I don't feel very good." I emerged from my room after sleeping in until ten o'clock the next morning. It was November first, just three days until "Duck Day." I sat at the top of the stairs, grabbing my stomach. Somehow, my dark-blonde wavy hair had fallen out of the bun on the top of my head and into my eyes, but I didn't care.

"Mom?" I yelled.

"Hang on, Allie."

Mom's voice sounded like it was below me. In our game room.

Or should I say, soon-to-be-someone-else's-game-room.

It was in moments like these that I missed my brothers, Ryan and Cody. Ryan, the oldest one, married his high-school sweetheart, Brittany, two years ago, and moved to California because they were both offered teaching jobs in Santa Barbara. They're now considered the "West Coast Carroways," and the producers fly them in to be in the show once in a while. If they were here right now, Ryan would find a way to make me laugh about this house nightmare, and Brittany—well, Brittany would be the perfect big sister and just hug me.

If my brother, Cody, were here, he'd boobytrap the house or figure out the perfect prank to play on everyone to buy us some time. Or to get the buyers to change their minds.

I lowered my face to my knees.

Maybe I should call Cody at college and ask him to come home

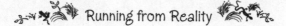

this weekend and help. It'll cost me some noogies, but it's a small price to pay . . .

"Allie? What's all the groaning about? Are you having an allergy attack?"

Mom came walking up the steps to greet me. She was wearing her grubby, light-gray sweats and oversized sweatshirt, and her blonde hair was piled on top of her head in a bun—but hers was staying.

I raised my head a few inches.

"How can you work out at a time like this, when I'm losing the only home I've ever known?"

Mom put her hands on her hips.

"Hey—at least you don't have to figure out how to weed out and pack twenty years of stuff. And I haven't been working out—I've been cleaning out the game room closet."

I straightened up.

"You didn't throw away any of the games, did you?"

"Allie, you never play them."

"But I'm comforted knowing they're there just in case."

Mom stepped up to the top of the steps, turned around, and sat down next to me. Then she lay down flat on her back.

"Help me, Lord! How am I going to move out of this house when my husband's out shootin' ducks every day?"

I copied her helpless pose and stared up at the ceiling.

"So, we're really moving out, then? This whole thing wasn't just a big Halloween prank?"

Mom reached over and grabbed my hand.

"Your dad and I are still praying about it, but if the offer looks as good as Ellen says it is, yes, we'll move out in thirty days—somehow. Kassie and Wayne already said we could move in with them. You and Kendall can share a room." Mom turned her head to look at me. "That should be fun, right?"

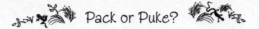

Songs swirled in my head as I imagined what my life would be like ²⁴/₇ with Kendall. It would be a musical, that's what. Playing air-guitar while dancing on the bed, composing love songs on the ukulele at night, and there would be the never-ending recording of cover songs for social media. Could I survive it?

Mom took a deep breath and sat up. She pulled me up and wrapped her arm around my shoulders.

"We have to remember that this is a good change. You're going to feel great living in our new house. So, we have a little inconvenience at first. We can do this, Allie-girl. We're Carroway women!"

"Umm, may I remind you, I'm just a Carroway *girl*. I've never moved even once before."

"But you've had to deal with much worse with all your health problems. Moving's nothing compared to that."

I smiled a little.

"If you say so."

Mom reached up to release her hair from her bun.

"Oh, hey—that reminds me. This morning the producers of the show called . . ."

My throat tightened.

"Yeeeeaaaaaah . . ."

She ran her fingers through her hair, and I watched in amazement as the locks fell into place like she just got out of a salon or something.

"And they had an idea. Last night, they got some great footage of the peanut fiasco . . ."

My heart started pounding.

"Yeeeeaaaaaah . . ."

Mom stopped with the hair fluffing.

"Why are you saying that?"

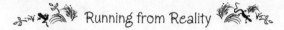

"Saying what?"

Mom crossed her arms. "Yeeeeeaaaaaaah."

"It's just that I already know what you're going to say."

"How do you know?"

"Because I know how this works. Go on."

Mom just stared and raised an eyebrow.

"Okay, Smart-Allie, the producers want to know if they can use some of the footage from last night in an upcoming episode so we can help people understand how serious food allergies are."

I stared back.

"You know, kind of like a . . ."

"Public service announcement?" I finished Mom's sentence for her.

She smiled. "Exactly."

I shot up on my feet.

"No!" I stamped my foot for effect, and more of the hair in my bun tumbled out.

Mom stood up next to me and put her hand on my shoulder.

"No? Really? Allie, I'm surprised by your reaction."

"What did you expect me to say? 'Sure, go ahead, because I don't mind being humiliated in front of millions of people?' Does everyone *always* have to know everything about us?"

"No, they don't." Mom took her hand and swept it in the air. "In fact, I don't see one single camera catching this glorious moment, do you?"

I dropped my face in my hands, breathed hard in and out, and then raised it back up again.

"I'm sorry. I . . . don't know what's wrong with me. I think I need some fresh air. Maybe a little . . ."

Run. Run, Allie!

"I'm gonna go for a run. Is that okay?"

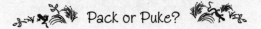

Mom gave me a hug. "It's fine with me, but take your inhaler." Mom started back down the steps, then turned. "We'll talk about the show thing when your dad gets back from the realtor's office. He went to find out more about this family who wants to buy our house without even looking at it."

CHAPTER 5

Lickety Split

I had changed out of PJs into my favorite coral sweats, and was running on the path next to the river for at least five minutes before I remembered that I'm a gymnast—not a runner. I stopped, put my hands on my knees, and attempted to catch my breath.

"I wish I had some of Emmy's energy."

I smiled as I remembered the little girl with the fragile bones who had asked me to pray for her.

Lord, help her not to run if it's going to hurt her. Help her grow strong so she can do whatever you've created her to do.

I sat down cross-legged in the plush grass next to the path, pulled up a thick blade, and began to rip it apart when my phone buzzed inside my pink wrist pack.

I pulled it out and looked at the screen.

It was a text from Lola.

> I heard about your house!!!!!!!!!!!! What are you going to do?????????????

You can always count on Lola to feel your pain, but sometimes she comes up with new woes you haven't considered. She buzzed again:

> Are you really going to share a room with Kendall??????????? You know how much she sings!!!!!!!!!!!!! You can share a room with Ruby and me!!!!!!!!!

I texted her back.

Too many !!!!!!s and ?????s.

My phone rang. Lola's name flashed on the caller id.
I answered.
"I'm sitting here staring at the river and ripping grass."
"Oh, you poor thing!"
"I don't know what else to do." I pulled up a few more blades
and threw them into the wind.
"Let's meet at the Lickety Split."
"Uh . . . it's still under construction."
"Yeah, I know. We can meet at the bottom of the steps. I'll
text the other cousins and we'll see you there in ten minutes."

I heard a click on the other end. There was no point in pro-
testing. Lola was the fastest texter in Louisiana, so I was sure
that the cousins were already on their way.

I stood and brushed the grass off myself, put my phone
back in my pack, and decided to cartwheel my way to the
Split. It seemed fitting—considering my life was turning me in
circles . . . again.

The Lickety Split is the name of our soon-to-be Carroway
Cousin Clubhouse. It's a replacement for our old clubhouse—
the Diva Duck Blind. It was pink and purple and glittery, like a
princess castle. The thing was decades old—my dad and his
brothers used to play in that same clubhouse when they were
kids. There were only two problems with the Diva Duck Blind.
One, it wasn't an inviting place for boy cousins, and recently we
got one named Hunter. Two, the place was full of mold which
was slowly choking me.

So, we tore it down, and started over, with Hunter drawing
up new plans with an architect and overall handyman genius

named Mr. Dimple, who happened to be hanging up in the tree when I cartwheeled over.

"Helloooo down there, Allie Carroway!"

"Hi, Mr. Dimple! How's the Lickety Split coming along?"

Mr. Dimple climbed down the old pink and purple steps.

"Well," Mr. Dimple took off his work gloves and slapped them on his work pants to release the dirt. "I'd like to say it's being true to its name, but it's more like the 'Lickety Slow' at the moment. But that's how it is when you're building a foundation. We gotta make sure it's solid up there. It may seem like nothin's happenin', but you'll see, all of a sudden you'll have yourself a clubhouse."

"Well, if it's done before my new house, I might have to move in."

Mr. Dimple chuckled. "Well, the Split's gonna have some good square footage, but I'd still recommend you stay in your old house until the new one is done."

"That was the idea, but my parents got an offer last night. If they accept it, we're out in thirty days."

"Whoa! Do the buyers know that's right in the middle of duck-huntin' season?"

"They might not, but my dad is very aware."

"I hope to shout."

"Huh?"

"Oh, that's just an old phrase that means 'You better believe it.' My daddy used to say it all the time. You see, sometimes my mama would give him a rough time about goin' out after ducks, day in and day out . . ."

Mr. Dimple is the friendliest, most talkative man in my whole town. If you've got a few hours to chat, you're in luck, because Mr. Dimple does too. The trick comes when you don't have much time, and you have to think of a way to move out

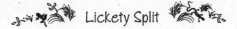

of the conversation without appearing rude. Thankfully for me, right at that moment, my cousins came running up the hill.

"I'm sorry, Mr. Dimple. I've gotta go. I have an important meeting."

He put his hand out. "Say no more, I understand how important it is for young folk to connect. I was about to take a break and go pick up some supplies anyway. You'll be seein' some real progress soon, I promise."

Mr. Dimple smiled and gathered up some of his tools.

"Thanks for working so hard on it," I said.

"It's a pleasure, Miss Allie." He started down the hill toward his truck, waving at Kendall, Hunter, Lola, and Ruby as he walked by.

"Hey, Allie! You lived!" Hunter's curly blonde hair bobbed on top of his head as he ran up the hill. He wore an oversized green T-shirt and long black basketball shorts, and carried his white bucket, which was usually filled with snacks, duct tape, and other random boy things. The three girls followed, and Ruby swung a basket which I hoped contained her famous chocolate-chip cookies.

Lola ran up to me, grabbed my hand, and squeezed it.

"You're not alone," she said. "We're behind this a hundred percent."

"Behind what?"

"Us taking a break from the show. Kendall told us everything. You're moving, I'm tired of wearing camo, and next week's scenes call for lots of it. It's duck-hunting season, you know."

I turned to Ruby.

"Are those cookies?"

Ruby smiled, and fiddled with the long, red braid that hung in front of her right shoulder.

"Yes, they are. Guaranteed nut free!"

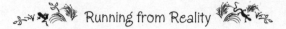

"Perfect." I reached out for the basket, and Ruby handed it to me. I looked up at the construction in the tree. "I wish the Lickety Split was ready. We could use a secret meeting place right now."

Hunter plunked down in the grass, and brought out a bag of gummy worms to munch on. He also pulled out a crumpled piece of paper.

"So, since I'm new to the family, I need you all to explain *this*."

We sat down in a circle, and Hunter held up the paper so we could see the written part. It said, "Hunter's Duck Season Chores."

Lola groaned. "Oh, no. The lists are out. We're doomed."

"Let me see that." Kendall took the list from Hunter and began to read it out loud. "Take out trash. Mow lawn. Sweep garage. Pull weeds. Rake leaves . . . Hey, that's on my list too!" She smacked the paper with the back of her hand.

I crossed my arms. "It's gonna be on all of our lists, people. The leaves never take a break around here."

"But, I don't get it," Hunter said. "These are all Dad's jobs. I help him when I can, but they aren't on my official chore list."

"Well, they are now, little brother, because Dad's about to disappear into Duckland."

"Disappear? You mean I won't see him at all?" Hunter frowned.

Ruby patted him on the shoulder.

"You'll get to see him a little. When I start to really miss my dad, I set my alarm for four in the morning, and I go eat cereal with him before he leaves."

"Four in the morning?" Hunter popped a worm in his mouth and chewed a little. "Isn't that still night?"

"It might as well be," Lola said.

"We'll get to film an episode with them out in the duck blind." Ruby was still trying to spin this as a good thing.

"Get to?" Lola threw her hands up in the air. "You mean we *have* to. And *that's* not the worst thing. More camo."

"And I don't like the smell out there," Kendall added.

"What does it smell like?" Hunter asked.

"Dirt and sweaty boys," Lola said.

Hunter sniffed his underarm. "I'm used to that, but do we have to go?" Hunter passed the worm bag around the circle.

"Yeah, at least a couple of times," I said. "The producers like to show us hunting with our dads."

"I hate hunting." Hunter slumped and popped a green worm in his mouth.

"Remember last year when that snake slithered up next to me, and I screamed on camera?" Ruby shook her head.

"*Remember*?" Lola dangled an orange gummy in front of Ruby's face. "It made history! Fan Favorite number five. People still talk about that."

"And I'm still embarrassed by it." Ruby blushed.

"I totally get the embarrassing part," I said. "The camera was rolling last night during my peanut scare, and they want to use it as a public service announcement to help people understand food allergies."

"I knew it! Didn't I just tell you that last night?"

"Yes, Kendall."

"We need to stop the madness," Kendall pounded her legs with her fists. "What's gonna happen when we all start dating? Are they gonna follow us around with cameras to try to catch our first kiss?"

"Eww," Ruby said. "I'm only ten. I'm not kissin' anyone!"

Hunter grinned. "Maybe if we just ask nicely, they'll take us out of the show."

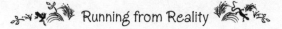

"Won't work," I said. "We're Carroways. The show's always been about our whole family."

"Well, there must be a way for us to share our concerns." Ruby took another bite of a cookie.

"We need some privacy and a break," Kendall spoke in her fake British accent and flipped her hair.

"We're not clueless kids anymore," Lola said. "We've got issues."

We all sat there for a minute, eating cookies and chomping on worms—like clueless kids.

Then an idea hit me.

"Hey—what if we went on strike?"

My cousins looked at me funny, and Hunter scratched his head. "What does that mean?" he asked.

"I was studying about it in history. When employees are unhappy, they all stop working at once, which causes a bunch of chaos, and then the bosses have to listen to them."

"Does it work?" Ruby asked.

"It did for the postal workers in 1970."

"Well, then," Kendall stood up and dug her fists into her hips. "I think we should go on strike."

"I agree," Lola stood and linked arms with Kendall. "How do we do it?"

"I'm not sure on all the details," I said. "But I know you have to make some signs. Then you march around and don't work until something happens."

"Like we get grounded?" Ruby said.

"Yeah," Hunter added. "I don't want to get in trouble."

"I don't think we'll get in trouble," I said. "As long as we stick together. That's the most important part of a strike. They need us. I mean, who's gonna rake all those leaves over the next few weeks?"

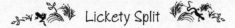

"I hate raking," Kendall said.

I looked around at our Lickety Split construction site. "We've got a bunch of scrap wood in that pile over there. Wanna make some signs?"

"Ruby and I'll go home and get some paint," Lola said.

"I have a hammer and nails in my bucket." Hunter reached in. "And duct tape."

"Perfect. We've got all afternoon, so we should be ready to strike before the meal scene we're filming tonight out at Mamaw and Papaw's."

"Oh, boy," Ruby cracked a couple of knuckles. "I'm getting a little nervous."

"Don't worry, Ruby," Hunter said. "Allie knows what she's doing."

Hearing Hunter say that made *me* nervous. After all, I only got a C on that history test about all the striking. I do remember that the strike went well for the postal carriers, but not for the railroad workers . . . or was it steel or coal workers? Hmmm. I was sure that a Carroway had never tried to go on strike, or I would have heard that story.

This was going to be an interesting night. And the cameras would be rolling.

This could turn out to be fan favorite moment number one.

CHAPTER 6

On Strike

My heart raced as we drove up the road toward my grand-parents' house near the Ouachita River. My cousins and I had wrapped our newly painted "strike signs" in a black tarp and stashed them in the back of our SUV. We'd decided where to march—outside, right in front of my grandparents' kitchen window. We just didn't know exactly *when* we should do it.

"We'll play it by ear," Lola had said.

Right now, as we drove up and parked, I wasn't feeling it at all.

"Allie, you've been quiet this whole drive. Are you okay?" Mom unbuckled her seatbelt and turned back to check on me in the second seat.

"I'm fine," I said, and I gathered my jacket and wrist pack, and headed out the door, up the steps to my grandparents' porch. Judging by the absence of vehicles, I figured we were the first ones here.

Mamaw's two dogs, Barney with the black spots, and his white poofball-sidekick, Andi, ran up and jumped on the screen door to greet us.

"Get down, you two!" Mamaw came to the door. "Barn-dog, you're teachin' Andi bad tricks."

Andi came to the Carroway family from the animal shelter just a few weeks earlier, right after a bad storm ripped through Louisiana, trapping me, Hunter, Lola, Ruby, and Kendall out-side in a flood with a gator. If it hadn't been for Hunter and his

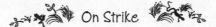

silly duct tape, we might not have survived to meet the little rascal.

Mamaw threw the screen open, and wrapped me up in a big hug.

"How's my sweet Allie doin' today? You gave us a real scare last night."

Poor Mamaw. I'm about to give you a little more grief tonight.

"I guess I gotta stop sneaking snacks under the table."

Mamaw pulled away, looked me in the eyes, and winked.

"Now, if you're ever hungry and need a snack, you just come and ask me. You know I always have somethin' in my purse. That caterin' food is awful."

A delicious aroma filled the air.

"Mamaw, are *you* cooking dinner tonight?"

"You better believe it, honey. I made gumbo! We'll be able to act like the food's delicious if it really is, don't ya think?

I love Mamaw's gumbo. How were we supposed to go on strike now?

I heard engine rumbles, so I poked my head out the screen door to see Lola and Ruby's family drive in, followed by Kassie and Wayne's. They pulled their trucks in next to each other, and my cousins piled out and ran up to the porch.

"Meet at the swing!" Kendall yelled out, and they ran past the door toward the side porch—our favorite place where we've had lots of sleepovers with Mamaw.

"Now y'all be careful out there!" Mamaw yelled. "Some things are still messed up from the storm."

"I'll be right back," I said, and I escaped out the door with Barney and Andi on my heels.

"Are you ready for this?" Kendall leaned over the railing looking out at the river in front of Mamaw and Papaw's house. "When do we get the signs?"

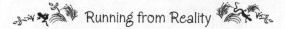

"Mamaw made gumbo for the meal scene," I said, and everyone gasped.

"I love gumbo." Hunter breathed in deep and rubbed his belly.

"If we go on strike, do we get to eat?" Ruby asked from her comfortable seat on the covered canvas swing.

"Depends on how it all goes down," Lola said.

Right then, Papaw Ray came out to meet us.

"It's a lot drier than the last time you rascals were here. You shoulda seen the junk that washed down the hills onto the riverbanks."

I wanted to ask Papaw if he had seen a gator with his mouth closed with duct tape. Hunter had done it. He didn't want to, and it was the scariest moment of our entire lives, but the ugly reptile had pinned Ruby up against a tree, and duct tape was the only weapon he had on him at the time. We didn't tell the adults all about our frightening adventure, since it was part of an initiation to welcome Hunter into the family and earn him access to our new Lickety Split clubhouse.

"Caught any crawdads lately?" Hunter pointed down to the steel nets that lay on the ground just in front of Mamaw's prayer bench in the front of the house.

"Naw—too busy gettin' ready for duck season. The fun all starts in three days, you know."

"Oh, yeah, we know." Hunter looked back at us and winked.

"We've got the chore list to prove it," Kendall said.

Papaw laughed. "A little extra work'll toughen you city-kids up. Make y'all appreciate what your dads do around the house."

A large black truck pulling a cargo trailer rumbled up the road, causing dirt to fly behind the mud tires.

"Film crew's here," Papaw said. "Time to get to work. At least we got some good food tonight. Your Mamaw made gumbo and

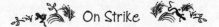

homemade biscuits. And mac and cheese for you, Allie-girl, since you had such a bad time last night."

"Yum," I said.

Papaw pointed toward our group. "So, don't y'all be late, you hear?"

Another SUV pulled up the road which held Kendall and Hunter's older siblings, and a few of our little kid cousins. This scene was gonna be big—one way or another.

"Hey, Hunter! Wanna play Frisbee?" Lola and Ruby's little brother Chase ran up the walk waving at us.

"Yes, but later!" Hunter turned back to look at us girls. "What are we gonna do?"

"It's now or never," I said. "As soon as they all go in the house, let's get the signs."

My hands turned clammy and I grew short of breath as I ran down the steps with my cousins and threw open the tailgate of our SUV.

No time for inhalers now.

"Where's *my* sign?" Kendall wrestled with the black plastic, and grabbed her sign that said "Raking" with a big circle around it and a slash through it.

"Here's yours, Lola." Hunter handed Lola hers, that read "Ducks = No Fun."

Ruby's just said "Carroways on Strike."

And I had two. One said "Privacy, Please!" and the other said "Run from Reality."

Hunter's said "Cousin Power."

"Okay, people," I said, "let's proceed to the marching area.

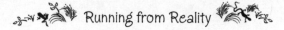

When we hear the dinner bell, ignore it. Make them come out and find us."

"I'm scared," Ruby's sign shook a little as she tried to hold it up.

"Just think," Kendall said. "This is gonna keep my first kiss off the TV."

Ruby shook her head. "Gross."

The November sun seemed extra hot, or maybe it was nerves causing me to sweat. We ran to the marching area and formed a circle. Then we started marching. For a few minutes, it was quiet, like no one was even home in the house. And then the dinner bell rang.

Hunter groaned. "I'm getting hungry."

"Me too," I said. "But we gotta stay strong."

Why did Mamaw have to make mac and cheese?

"Keep marchin', Hunter," Kendall said. "Or I'll make you rake my half of the leaves."

A few minutes later, we heard the squeak of the screen door. Mom and Dad came walking down the steps, both with their arms crossed. Following close behind were Kassie and Wayne—Hunter and Kendall's parents, then Josiah and Janie—Lola and Ruby's parents. And right behind them were Mamaw and Papaw. Papaw chewed on a steaming, buttered biscuit. When they all got down to us, they formed a circle around our marching circle. They didn't say a thing—just stared us down.

I looked up toward the house and saw the older and younger cousins' faces crowded in the window, staring out at us too.

"Keep marching,'" I whispered, though everyone heard me.

Ruby tripped over a stick and dropped her sign, so we had to stop marching for a second. Hunter helped her pick it up.

"Didn't y'all hear the dinner bell?" Papaw grinned when he wasn't gnawing on his biscuit.

I cleared my throat, stood up a little straighter, and threw my shoulders back.

"Yes, we did," I said. "But, Papaw, we're on strike."

"On strike from what?" Dad asked.

"The show," I said. "That's why we're not coming in to eat."

"You're not gonna eat my gumbo?" Mamaw wiped her hands on her apron. "I made it with love for all of my children and grandchildren."

"I want to eat the gumbo," Hunter said.

"That's my boy." Uncle Wayne reached for Hunter's sign, but he pulled it back.

"But we can't eat it right now. Not till the strike's over."

"And will that be over in the next couple of minutes?" Aunt Kassie glanced down at her watch.

"We should get the film crew out here for this," Uncle Wayne said.

"No!" Kendall yelled. "That's what we're striking against! We're not kids anymore, and we're tired of being filmed all the time."

"Ducks = No Fun?" Uncle Josiah gasped and pointed to Lola's sign. "Whose child are *you*?"

"Sorry, Dad." Lola looked down at the ground. "It's how I feel."

"Here's the issue," I said. "We can't go anywhere without people snapping pictures of us, and now we're supposed to film, do homework, *and* do extra chores because of duck season. Plus, my family has to move in thirty days."

I started a chant.

"We need a break! We need a break! We need a break!"

Eventually all the cousins joined in.

And all the adults went back in the house for dinner.

CHAPTER 7

Demands and Deals

W e need a break! We need a break! We need a break!"
I continued the chant, but louder, since everyone we wanted to hear this was inside now.

"Hey, Allie, can we take a break right now? My feet are tired." Ruby set her sign on the ground and went to sit down on Mamaw's prayer bench. "I don't think the strike's working."

Kendall did the same. "Yeah, I guess I expected a little more reaction from the adults."

"At least we didn't get grounded," Lola said.

"Yet," added Ruby.

"I think they're in there eating, and that might be a good thing. Food puts people in a good mood." Hunter set his sign down, and leaned against the back of the bench, looking up at the house. "I hope they leave some food for us."

"How long should we stay out here?" Ruby asked.

"Till they come out and meet our demands," Kendall said.

"I don't think that's gonna happen," Lola hung her head.

"Our parents are as stubborn as us." Ruby closed her eyes and rested her head on Lola's shoulder.

We waited in silence for another five minutes or so, and then Papaw Ray came out of the screen door, with a pad of paper and pen in his hand. He was still grinning.

He walked down to us at the prayer bench.

"Can one of you move so this old man can sit?"

Ruby slid off.

"Okay, then." Papaw Ray sat down and gave us each a long look. "You're on strike. What are your demands?"

"We don't want to wear camo anymore," Lola said.

Papaw didn't even uncap his pen.

"Request denied. Next?"

"No more raking leaves," Kendall stomped her foot.

Papaw narrowed his eyes.

"Request denied. Next?"

"We don't want to be on the show anymore." I ventured in big with that one.

Papaw raised his eyebrows and stared right at me.

"Allie-girl, are you sure about that? What if God has called you to be in the show to bless folks and shine your light in the world?"

"Uh . . . I haven't given that much thought."

"I know you haven't, so for now I'm gonna deny that request too. You kids got anything else? This is weak sauce."

"Umm . . ." Hunter waded in. "Can we maybe just take a break? We've got homework and now we have a bunch of extra chores. And Allie has to move in with us pretty soon. We're kinda stressed."

Papaw leaned back on the bench. One side of his mouth turned up.

"Okay, now there's a reasonable request."

A butterfly woke up somewhere in my stomach and flew around.

"Really? You think we could take a break from the show? I'm so tired of people knowing everything and taking pictures and videos of everything. I just want to be anonymous for a change."

Papaw stroked his beard. "I think that can be arranged. We've got some holidays comin' up, don't we? Aren't you kids outta school sometime near Thanksgivin'?"

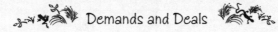

"Yeah," Kendall said. "But we always have to film that traditional 'live' show where we do the pilgrim play and chase wild turkeys around. We're growin' up, Papaw. Can't we do somethin' else?"

We watched as Papaw scribbled some notes on his paper. Then he finally looked up.

"How about we scrap the turkey show, and I send y'all on a vacation instead?"

I was pretty sure my ears were full of wax, because I thought I heard Papaw say he was going to send us on a vacation.

"A Vay. . . . cay . . . shun?" Lola looked like she might faint right there on the bench.

"Yep. I'll send you wherever you want to go for a week."

"Disneyland?" Ruby jumped up and down.

"Except Disneyland, because we just went to Disney World a few months ago, and you got lost, young lady. But I could send y'all to California to visit Ryan and Brittany."

"Can we go to Malibu?" Lola's always talked about living there and doing nothing but painting and playing beach volleyball.

"I want to go to the La Brea Tar Pits!" Hunter's eyes bulged out of his head. "I *need* to see dinosaur bones."

I held my hand out. "It's a deal, Papaw."

Papaw shook his head. "Not yet, Allie-gator. I'm not done negotiatin' just yet."

"What are you talkin' about?" Kendall asked.

"Well," Papaw leaned back again. "During a strike, people make deals. You give some things and you get some things. I'm willin' to give you a vacation, but you gotta give me somethin'."

"What?" I realized I was still holding my "Run from Reality" sign, so I lowered it to the ground.

"You give me your promise that you won't take *any* video or

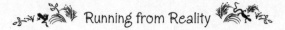

photos while you're on your trip, and that you won't tell a single livin' soul about *anything* that happens while you're gone. It'll be just like you say you want things to be—totally private. It's time you feel what that's like."

"That's ridiculous!" Kendall huffed and puffed. "What if I meet one of my favorite singers in Hollywood? Are you sayin' I can't take a selfie?"

"That's what I'm sayin.' Take it or leave it, but those are my demands."

We were all silent for a moment. No pictures or video. No bringing back stories. No one would know where we'd been or what we'd been up to.

It sounded perfect to me.

"Deal!" I yelled, which made Ruby jump.

I looked at the other cousins.

"Well, if it's okay with all of you."

Lola smiled.

"I can't wait to see a Malibu sunset."

I held up an index finger. "But no pictures, right?"

She cocked her head and looked at Papaw. "Could I paint it?"

Papaw stroked his beard and thought a minute.

"I wouldn't be against that. It will give you time for quiet reflection."

"Then I'm in," Lola said.

"Me too. I've always wanted to eat at In-N-Out Burger." It doesn't take too much to make Ruby happy.

"I'm totally in," Kendall said.

"Me too." Hunter looked up toward the house and rubbed his belly. "Can we eat now?"

Papaw grinned. "What makes you think there's any food left?"

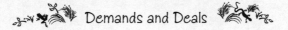

"Mamaw cooked, right?" I tossed my sign to the ground. "There should be enough for the whole town."

Papaw reached out and messed up my hair.

"You got that right. Now get in there and fill yourselves up. Then we'll plan your Run from Reality."

CHAPTER 8

Separation Anxiety

Three weeks later, after we had done all the duck chores we could stand, our whole family came to see us off at the Monroe Regional Airport.

"Ray, I can't believe I let you talk me into sending my baby off alone on an airplane." Mom shook her head and hugged me so tight I could hardly breathe.

"Look around," Papaw gestured to all five of us. "They have each other. I arranged a guide to meet 'em in Dallas if they need help. And when they get to the end, Ryan and Brittany will be there to pick 'em up. And those two are the most responsible individuals on the planet."

I tried to pull away from Mom. "We'll be fine. We have three hours to find the gate, and we'll be inside the terminal. What could happen?"

"We're Carroways," Kendall said. "Anything could happen. That's what makes it fun."

Mom shook her head. "I don't know . . ."

"Maggie," Dad said, "the airline knows they're comin.' The Dallas airport has good signage. They can read. We gotta let 'em go sometime."

"Passengers of flight 1145 going to Dallas-Fort Worth, please proceed to security check-in if you have not already done so."

I couldn't believe this was happening.

We all grabbed our carry-on backpacks and turned toward the security line, but Papaw stopped us.

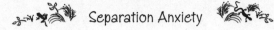

"Hold up, rascals. We need to make a trade." He reached into his camo bag and pulled out what looked like phones.

"What are those?" Hunter asked. "They look exciting."

"These are called burner phones. I have one for each of you to use only for this trip. I've programmed in every family member's phone number, and you all have access to calling and texting."

"Let me see that," Kendall said, and she grabbed one of the phones and flipped it open. "Where are all the apps?"

"No apps," Papaw said. "And no cameras."

I think all our mouths dropped open at once.

"Why do y'all look like a bunch of frogs waitin' for flies? We have a deal, right? These phones will help keep you honest." Papaw held out his open bag. "Okay, let's have your phones."

It was a painful exchange. Our cool phones with the personalized covers and carefully chosen wallpaper and apps for black nerdy flip phones that did nothing but call 9–1–1 and our parents. Nice.

"All passengers of flight 1145 for Dallas-Fort Worth, proceed to the security line if you have not already done so."

Mom hugged me again, tighter. Dad shook his head and pried her away from me.

She knelt and looked me in the eyes.

"Be smart. Don't talk to strangers. Call me as many times as you want. Call me when you get to Dallas."

"Oh, brother." Dad shook his head. He pulled me away from Mom and gave me a hug. "Have a good time bein' anonymous. Y'all take care of each other."

I smiled. "We will. We're Carroways."

The other cousins' parents were having a hard time pulling away too.

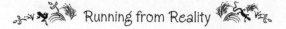
"Enough with the clingin'," Papaw Ray said. "Let 'em experience life in the real world."

Then he shooed us off, and we found ourselves in the security line alone—just us kids. Well, and a bunch of other people too.

A light flashed in my peripheral vision. Someone taking a photo. I rolled my eyes and leaned over to talk to Kendall.

"As soon as I get to California, my hair is going up in a hat, and I will no longer respond to the name Allie Carroway."

"I feel ya, girl. I brought five pairs of sunglasses, a bunch of scarves, and some hair color. I'm going red for a week."

"Red? Like Ruby?" I pointed to Ruby's harvest-orange colored hair.

"Nah. Red like an apple!"

"Do you think Ryan and Brittany will go for that?" I tried to imagine for a second what I would look like as a platinum blonde.

"I'm not gonna ask 'em," Kendall said. "It's just a temporary color wash. It'll be gone in a week."

Lola leaned in to join the conversation.

"My pink streak is changing to a turquoise streak in the morning. To match the color of the Pacific Ocean."

I turned to Hunter. "And how are you going to alter your appearance? Get yourself a mohawk?"

Hunter laughed. "Nope. I'm just gonna stay me. But I'm gonna be fast. Just fly in and out of places. Like a flash of light. No one will be able to focus on my face long enough to identify it."

"I won't have to do a thing except change out of denim. People will be confused by that." Ruby doesn't own anything that isn't jeans. She even has jeans pajamas.

"Excuse me." A business man behind us held his hand

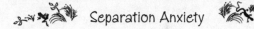

toward the young female TSA agent who was now staring at our group. "You're holding up the line."

"Oops. Sorry." I moved forward, handing the agent my boarding pass and passport.

"I don't have a driver's license, so I hope this works."

"You're fine, Allie," the TSA agent said. She scanned my boarding pass. "You can leave your shoes on. Enjoy your flight. And by the way, I love your show." She smiled and handed back my papers.

"Oh . . . uh . . . okay. Thank you, ma'am." I smiled and stepped forward to the scanning area. I heaved my giant backpack into a gray bin and pushed it onto the conveyor belt.

"Walk through the arch, please," a dark-haired middle-aged man in a suit said. He looked like he might be everyone's boss. "You can wait for your baggage over there." He pointed to the end of the conveyor that was just past some officials holding scanning wands.

Just about then, my backpack beeped.

"We've got a knife over here, Rod." A girl sitting near a computer called the boss-guy over.

"Did you bring a knife with you?" he asked me.

"What? No! I . . . Oh, wait a minute, maybe I did. But it's just a little pink camo folding one my dad gave me. I forgot it was in there. He-he. Sorry."

The girl held it up. "This can't go. You can return to the check-in desk and have it added to your luggage, or you can surrender it."

"Um, I'll just surrender it. I have a few more of those at home for, um . . . gutting fish and other gross stuff you wouldn't believe."

The lady laughed.

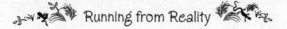

"Yeah, I would. I watch the show. I'm sorry I have to take it from you, but rules are rules."

"It's okay. If you have a daughter, you can give it to her and tell her it's from Allie Carroway."

She nodded and grinned. "I do, and I will. Thank you!"

"You're welcome."

"Move along, felon." Kendall pushed me in the back. "I can't believe you brought a knife! Man, if only I could have taken a photo of that to put on social media. Allie Carroway brings a knife on a plane. You got any other surprises you'd like to tell me about?"

"None that I know of."

"Good. We're trying to stay anonymous, remember?"

"I'll try harder."

But it got harder in Dallas.

...

CHAPTER 9

Layover Lunch Bag

The flight to the Dallas-Fort Worth airport was peaceful, but crunched. We sat in the very back row of the airplane—in the seats that don't recline because the bathroom is right behind you.

"I guess Papaw wanted us to travel like 'normal' people," Lola said.

Usually when our family flies, we go in a jet that the network owns, or we get first class seats. Once we had to fly coach, but we were in the "roomier legroom" seats. The seats in this plane had no legroom, and no back room! Just bathroom. And since most of the people in the plane were from our town, they made a point to say hello on their way to do their business. I started to wonder if they really had to go, or if they just wanted to see the Carroway cousins shoved like sardines in the back of a plane.

"Fresh air!" Hunter held up his arms and turned in a circle as we deplaned in Dallas. "I smell burgers!"

I pulled my boarding pass out of my backpack to look at the time of our next flight.

"We have to get to terminal B, gate 57 by three forty-five. That's three hours from now. I say, let's eat."

"There's a McDonalds." Ruby pointed toward the golden arches, and Kendall scrunched up her nose.

"McDonald's? Can't we find somethin' more refined? Or somethin' that reflects the Texas culture?"

"Let's check the directory." Ruby ran up to the lighted sign in the middle of the walkway. She pushed her finger on the glass. "They have Taco Bell, Starbucks, Subway . . . Hmmm. All the stuff we have at home."

"How about this?" Lola pointed to one a few lines down. "Cowboy Chow Down. It's in Terminal C."

"Sounds great to me," Hunter said.

"But, people, it's in terminal C. We're in terminal A now, and we have to get to terminal B for our flight."

"But I really want to chow down, Allie!" Hunter said.

The aroma of McDonald's fries was about to drop me to the floor. I didn't know if I had the energy to find terminal C until I downed some salt and fat.

"Okay, let me get some fries, and then we can make the journey to the chow place."

"I want some food too," Ruby said. "I'll go with you, Allie."

"And we'll just wait here and maybe check out the gift shop." Kendall plopped her stuff on a bench that was across from a large TV that was showing the Dallas Cowboys game.

"Can you get me a couple of cookies?" Hunter asked. "I'd like to start my chow down early."

"Whatever you want," I said.

Ruby and I hoisted our backpacks on our backs and jostled our way into the line for McDonalds. The weight of my pack tilted me forward, and I stepped on the back of a teenaged boy's canvas surf shoe, giving him a flat.

"Dude!" He reached down to grab his ankle.

When he turned to look back at me, my face flushed. He was a cutie. A little taller than me, strong shoulders, smooth sandy blonde hair, and a tan face, except for a little sunburn peel on his nose.

"I'm so sorry," I said. "My backpack made me do it."

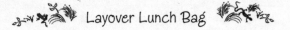

He smiled with some extra-white teeth. Then he reached down and pulled the back of the shoe up. "It's cool."

Ruby giggled a little, and I jammed my elbow in her side.

"Your face and neck are red," she whispered.

I reached up to touch my cheeks with my cold, clammy hands, and I waited behind the boy with the faded blue T-shirt that said *Surf & Son Summer* on it. He also wore tan cargo shorts, and no socks with those surf shoes. The heather gray backpack he carried in his hand almost matched mine.

The McDonald's line moved forward, and I watched my step this time.

Maybe he'll turn around again. No, wait a minute. I don't want him to turn around again.

Ruby interrupted my conflicting thoughts.

"Allie, I have to go to the bathroom. Can you order me a hamburger Happy Meal?"

I kept staring at the boy's back.

"Allie?" Ruby nudged me.

"What? Did you say something?"

Ruby pushed money into my hand.

"I gotta go. Hamburger Happy Meal, fries, and a Coke. Any toy will be fine."

Then she giggled and took off.

"Take Kendall or Lola with you!" I shook my head. That girl could get lost in her own house. What would I tell Aunt Janie if I lost Ruby?

"Are you having a good trip so far?"

The voice sounded far off, but I soon realized it was right next to me. Mystery Boy had turned around and was looking at me with his rich, azure blue eyes.

I cleared my throat.

"Yes. So far. I mean, it's just the beginning . . ."

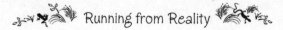

He kept looking.

"That's cool. Mine's just ending. I've got one more flight . . ."

"Next guest, please."

How rude for that McDonald's employee to interrupt such an important conversation!

"Oops. Gotta go." Blue Eyes stepped to the counter, and I strained to hear what he would order off the menu.

"Uh, let's see, I'm pretty hungry, so I'll have two Quarter Pounders with cheese, a large fry, three cookies . . . no wait a minute, make that one Quarter Pounder, and an order of chicken nuggets. I'll take a medium Coke too, and cookies. Yeah, three cookies."

The employee poked his computer and then looked up.

"You said three cookies twice. So, do you want six cookies total, or just the three?"

Surfer Dude began digging in his pockets.

"Wow—I really said it twice? Well, I guess that means I'm meant to have six then."

He continued to dig, and he finally pulled out a brown leather wallet.

"That'll be $15.69," the employee said.

Surfer Guy held up a card. "Cool. I've been waiting to use this baby."

He swiped the McDonald's gift card and waited.

After a few seconds, the employee shook his head.

"It's not going through. Try swiping it again."

My stomach did a little dance while he swiped and waited.

"It's not working," the employee said. "Would you like to use an alternate form of payment?"

"Oh, no, that's a bummer. Hang on, let me see what I have left of my cash."

He dug in a few more cargo pockets, and managed to pull

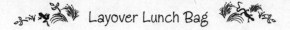

out some bills and a handful of change. He dumped it all out on the counter, and the employee shook his head as he began straightening out the bills and sorting out the coins.

"That's $12.40." He gathered the money, placed it in his cash drawer, and poked some more buttons. "You're $3.29 short. Would you like to eliminate one of your items?"

Before I could even think—I stepped forward, held out the five-dollar bill that was in my hand, and gave it to the cashier.

"Here. You can add this."

Surfer Boy held out both hands to try to stop the transaction, but the McDonald's employee was fast, and before we knew it, my new blue-eyed, surfer friend was getting change back.

"Dude, you didn't have to do that."

"It's okay, I had extra. Plus, you're a big guy, so you need the food."

What a dumb thing to say! Now he's going to think I noticed his muscles. Ugh!

"Well, that was a very nice thing to do."

"Next guest, please."

Another employee, a young woman with big blonde hair and a lot of eyeliner, smiled at me from behind her computer. I stepped forward, while keeping the Dude Guy—who was waiting for his order—in my peripheral vision.

"What can I get you today, darlin'?"

"I'll take a large order of fries, please."

"You wanna drink with that, honey?"

"No, thank you."

"Okay, sugar, that'll be $2.49."

I reached in my pocket and pulled out three singles. I handed them to her, and she gave me change and a receipt with my order number on it. Then she leaned forward to talk to me.

"Maybe dreamy-boy over there will share some of his cookies with ya." Then she winked, and I'm sure I turned beet red.

I tried to cool my face with my freezing hands. All the blood must have rushed to my heart to keep it from stopping.

"Was there somethin' else you wanted, sweetie?"

"Um, no. Thanks. I'll . . . just . . . wait . . . there."

I pointed to the side a few feet over.

She nodded. "Yes, that's right."

I stepped aside, a foot away from the boy I just gave money to without his permission.

Try not to embarrass yourself further, Allie.

"One forty-six!"

That was the boy's number. He stepped forward to grab his bag of food, drink cup, and lots of cookies.

"Hey, thanks again." There he was. Talking to me.

Don't say anything dumb. In fact, don't say anything.

"Hey, I have something for you."

"For me?"

He held out some money. "Yeah. Your change."

I laughed, a little too hard. "Oh, yes, thanks." I held out my hand, and he dropped a couple of dollars and some warm coins into my hand.

He set his food down on the counter, and pulled his backpack off his back. He unzipped the main compartment. "I have something else too."

I said nothing, and watched as he pulled out a beat-up, brown lunch bag.

"I'm the last person in my group to give mine away, and I guess I've been extra picky about the person I'm supposed to give it to. But you have kind eyes, and since you just stepped up and helped me in a big way, I think you're the one."

He handed me the bag. I reached out and took it.

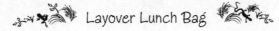

"Thank you," I said. "What's in here?"

He shrugged and one eyebrow went up.

"Everything you need."

"Nathan! Come on, dude! Our plane's boarding in ten!"

I turned around to see a fast-moving group of boys with backpacks carrying Taco Bell bags and gesturing for my surfer-friend to join them.

He gathered up his things.

"I gotta go. Thanks for making sure I didn't starve."

And then he disappeared in a sea of bobbing heads and wheeled carry-ons.

"One forty-seven!"

"Is that our order?" Ruby had returned, and she looked hungry.

I checked my receipt and stepped forward to get the bag of fries. And then I realized my mistake.

"That doesn't look like a Happy Meal," Ruby said.

I hung my head. "It's not. Ruby, I forgot to order your food."

And I just bought six cookies for a stranger and forgot to get some for Hunter!

"It was that boy, wasn't it?"

I nodded. "I'm really sorry."

Ruby sighed. "It's okay. I'll just get food at the Cowboy Chow place." She pointed to the crumpled-up lunch bag. "What's that?"

Right as she asked, the rest of my cousins showed up.

"This? Oh, it's just something that boy gave me."

"What boy?" Kendall asked.

"He was in front of me in line. I flatted his shoe and then paid for his lunch. He gave me this."

"Do you know what's in there?" Hunter stepped a little closer.

"No," I said.

"Throw it out! Quick! It could be a bomb!" Lola backed up several feet.

"Don't be ridiculous." I gathered my stuff and headed out toward the signs that said "Terminal C." My cousins followed.

"Allie, I'm serious!" Lola tried to stop me by grabbing my shoulder. "You can't just take a plain bag from someone in an airport!"

I stopped, and my cousins circled around me.

"Think, people. We're in a terminal. Whatever's in this bag had to get through security, and we already know that they're tough down there because they didn't even let me keep my little princess camo knife."

"So, are you gonna open it and let us see what's in there?" Kendall reached for the bag, but I pulled it away from her.

"No, I'm not. He said it was everything I need, so when I need something, I'll look."

Kendall rolled her eyes. "Man, he must have been cute."

I put one hand on my hip. "He was nice. And that's all I want to say. Now let's go get some chow."

CHAPTER 10

Terminal Pile-up

I love this Cowboy food!" Hunter popped a chili-fry into his mouth. "It was worth the walk."

The "walk" he spoke of was about a half-mile to the train, which took us to terminal C. And then it was a quarter-mile walk to the Cowboy Chow Down.

"Did you know that the Dallas-Fort Worth airport is larger than the island of Manhattan?" Hunter patted the front pocket of his backpack. "I read it in the Dallas tour book."

"You brought a Dallas tour book?" Kendall reached over and snatched one of Hunter's fries. "We're not visiting Dallas, ya know."

"We're in the Dallas airspace, so I call that visiting Dallas," Hunter said. "The Cowboys are on, and there are stars everywhere. I like to find out what I can about the places I visit."

"You know what, Hunter?" Lola pointed to a guy wearing a cowboy hat who was leaving the Cowboy Chow Down. "I think you should get one of them hats." She spoke with a Texas drawl. "I think it would look downright handsome on ya."

"That could be your disguise," I said. "It would be less tiring that running everywhere, trying to be blurry."

Hunter's eyes lit up. "Great idea! Let's find a cowboy store!"

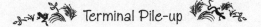

"Here's one." Ruby pointed to a name on the directory we found in terminal C.

"*Cowboy Up—the Place to Get the Gear.* I think they might have a hat," Lola said.

"But it's in terminal E!" I put my heavy backpack on the floor for a second to rest my shoulders. "That means . . ."

"We better get movin'!" Hunter said. "I'll take that for you, Allie!" Then he picked up my backpack and ran with it toward the sign that directed us to the train for terminal E.

"What time is our flight?" Lola asked.

"Four o'clock," I said. "We've got one hour."

"I'm sure that will be enough time," Ruby said. "If we don't run into any trouble."

We didn't run into trouble. We just ran into each other.

It was after we spent thirty minutes picking out and purchasing Hunter's hat. It was a fancy one—made of black felt with a four-inch brim, and a brown-braided band with silver detail. Hunter looked just like a cowboy when he put it on, except for the long basketball shorts.

"We can work on that," Lola said.

The problem wasn't in the picking, it was in the paying. The line was long, and every person in the line seemed to need additional customer service.

"We gotta hurry, people," I said.

And so we hurried. As soon as Hunter purchased his hat, we charged out of the store toward the train.

"The train for terminal B is way down there!" Lola huffed and puffed and tried to pull her backpack straps a little tighter.

"Look! There's a moving sidewalk," Hunter said. "If we run on that we can go lightspeed."

It seemed like the perfect idea, so we followed Hunter on. And we *were* going lightspeed, until our cowboy tripped and fell.

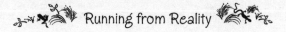

And Kendall slammed into Hunter.
And Lola jammed into Kendall.
And Ruby rammed into Lola.
And I completed the five-cousin pile-up.
And there was blood.

CHAPTER 11

Princess Patch-Up

My knees!" Hunter somehow managed to keep his hat on during the cousin crash, but not his knee skin. Blood dripped down his calves and into his socks.

"My hands are not much better." Kendall rubbed her bloodied palms onto her pant legs.

Lola inspected her elbows. "This is gonna hurt in the shower."

Ruby and I had a few scrapes on our arms and hands too.

People walking the opposite way next to the moving sidewalk held their hands to their mouths as they walked by. One lady yelled, "Are y'all alright? Do you need first aid?"

The answer was yes, but we didn't have time. If I just had some Band-Aids, I could get this beat-up crew to the gate to board the plane in time without them bleeding out.

"Let's get off this moving death belt and come up with a strategy," I said.

We exited at the next opening, which happened to be right in front of the doors for the terminal B train. The doors opened in seconds, and we piled on. People on the train gawked. "We had a little accident," I said to no one in particular. "But we'll be fine."

Ruby pulled a napkin out of her backpack, wetted it with her water bottle, and handed it to Hunter. "Here. You have blood all over, and you're scaring the children."

Hunter grimaced. "Thanks." And he began to wipe.

"We need to stop at a store and get some bandages," Lola said.

I looked down at my watch. "We don't have time."

I dug in my backpack to see if maybe I left Band-Aids in there and forgot—like I forgot the knife. I checked each pocket, but only found some mints, hand sanitizer, and a phone number written on a piece of paper. No idea whose it was.

And then I saw the lunch bag, and remembered my surfer-friend's words regarding its contents:

Everything you need.

"Hang on," I said. I kept the bag in the backpack, but unfolded the top. I felt a little silly, but I just had this expectant feeling that I couldn't explain.

When I opened the bag, I could hardly believe my eyes.

The item on top was a box of Band-Aids. Princess themed. Assorted sizes *and* princesses.

I wanted to hold the box up, jump around, and exclaim, "It's a lunch bag miracle, people!" But instead, I decided to keep it a secret.

"Here," I said, and I pulled the box out of the pack. "These should work."

"Do you have knee-sized ones?" Hunter was still using the water from Ruby to wash off his wounds.

I pulled out two big square ones and handed them to Hunter.

"I hope you don't mind Cinderella." I laughed a little. "At least your shorts are long enough to cover them up when you stand."

Hunter peeled off the wrapping and pulled the backing off the sticky part. He placed the Cinderella bandages on his knees, and then sighed.

"Feels better with the air not hitting them."

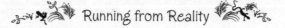

"I'll take The Little Mermaid," Kendall said. "She's a good singer, and tomorrow my hair will be the same color."

I handed her a few smaller Ariel strips for the cuts on her hands.

"Why do you have princess bandages?" Lola asked. "I thought you weren't a princess fan." She pulled out a couple of Snow Whites and slapped them on her elbows.

"I am now," I said.

A recorded voice came over the loud speaker.

"Arriving at terminal B in . . . twenty seconds . . ."

The train slowed, and people who were standing moved toward the double doors.

I checked my watch again.

"Okay, listen up. We don't have much time, so no getting food or stopping in shops. Watch the signs for gate 57 and make sure we all go the right direction together."

"I'll hang on to you," Ruby said, and she grabbed one of my backpack straps.

"Good thinking," I said.

"Arriving . . . terminal B . . ."

The train came to a halt and we all stood.

"I don't think we should run this time," Hunter said.

The doors opened, and right in front of us was a sign that showed gates 25–50 to the left, and gates 51–75 to the right.

Thank you, Lord.

Good thing Ruby was hanging onto me, because she tried to turn left.

"I'm glad it's not too far," Lola said.

I could see the sign for gate 57 up in the distance, and a line was forming to board.

Whew, we made it!

A thin, red-headed young man wearing wire-framed glasses and a gray suit came running up to us.

"Are you the Carroway children?"

We froze in place and said nothing.

His head turned left and right, and as he scanned all of us, he tap-tap-tapped his foot and closed his fingers together in the shape of a teepee.

"Well, of course you're the Carroways! I've seen the show!" He threw one hand up in the air.

The nervous guy then yelled to a girl at the desk who was on the phone. "I found them, Virginia!" Then he turned back to us and crossed his arms. "Where have you been for the last three hours? Your people have been calling."

"People?" I asked. "What people?"

"Well, here are a few names you might recognize." He started ticking names off on his fingers. "Papaw Ray, Maggie, Jake, Mamaw Kat . . ."

"Mamaw called?" Ruby smiled. "She gets lost a lot too, just like me."

He continued, "Wayne, Janie, and then there was that California Carroway named Ryan . . ."

"My brother called?" I smiled.

Virginia walked over to us.

"We need to get you kids boarded. Why didn't you wait for the guide when you got off your last flight?"

"Guide?" Lola scratched her head.

"Yes, that would have been *me*," Jittery Man said. "You were supposed to meet *me* at the desk when you got off the plane."

"Oh, yeah. I remember Papaw saying something about that." Kendall elbowed me. "What happened, Allie?"

I shrugged.

"I thought that was just if we needed help. Plus, fresh air

79

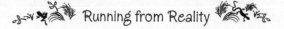

and McDonald's fries were calling. I'm sorry, um . . . what's your name?"

"Austin. The name's Austin. Like the town in Texas. But I almost became 'Austin—The Airline Employee Who Lost the Famous Carroway Children in Texas. Film at Eleven'."

"I'm really sorry," I said. "I guess we forgot about the whole guide thing."

Austin started talking to himself while he scanned the ceiling.

"It'll be an easy job, Austin. Just meet *five adolescents* at the gate and guide them over to terminal B. It'll be fun. They're reality stars. Shouldn't be any trouble at all . . . Yeah, right!" Austin shook his head, and huffed and puffed like he'd eaten too much hot sauce. Then he began batting the air in front of him, as if it were filled with blood-sucking gnats. Just when his face had reached the color of Lola's hair streak, he stopped, and stuck his face out from his neck.

"WHERE have you people been?"

"Terminal E," Hunter said.

"Yes, I can tell." Austin flicked the bill of Hunter's hat.

"And terminal C," Kendall added. "We were hungry."

Austin stuck out a finger. "Let me guess, the Chow Down?"

"It was really good," Lola said, and then she burped. "Excuse me."

"And now we're here at terminal, uh . . . which one is this?" Ruby asked.

"Terminal B," Austin said, and then he shook his head. "Just wondering, why didn't you visit terminal D too, just to make sure you toured the *entire* airport? Do you have something against the letter D?"

I tried to hide a laugh, but was unsuccessful.

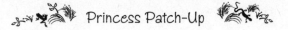

Hunter smiled, which told me he wasn't feeling this guy's stress at all.

"Is there something exciting in terminal D?"

"NO! There's nothing exciting *anywhere* in this airport! Got that? Next time—proceed to your gate. Don't pass go! Don't collect two-hundred dollars!"

He looked down at all our bandages.

"And *why* are you all cut up? Did you take a little trip to the rodeo, too, and do some bull riding?"

"Austin? The captain would like us to finish boarding this flight." Virginia had returned, and she handed Austin a plastic bottle of what looked like antacids. He poured a few out, popped them in his mouth, and started chomping.

Austin looked at us through narrowed eyes. "Well, you heard Virginia, it's time to board. Move along, adolescents." Austin led us right to the front of the boarding line and scanned our passes.

"Now, have a nice flight," he said, and he practically shoved us down the airwalk. "And, if you children have phones, you might want to call your family before you're in the air so they know you aren't dead."

I turned to wave at the poor guy.

"Thank you, sir. And once again, we are very sorry."

Austin said nothing as he turned around and stomped off.

"Working for the airlines must be stressful," Lola said.

"Sounds like he needs a little getaway too." Kendall snickered.

Hunter, who led our line down the aisle of the airplane, came to our row—twenty-two. Not as far back as the bathrooms, but still far back.

"Here we are, Cowgirls, seats A–E. I'll sit in seat D, since I have nothing against that letter."

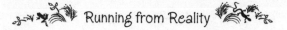

We all laughed. And then we laughed harder when Hunter ducked his head to get to the middle seat on the right side of the plane and the carry-on compartment knocked his hat off.

"Wait—I want the window seat so I can see Malibu." Lola picked up Hunter's hat, handed it to him, and then squeezed by.

"I'll take the aisle." Ruby pushed her backpack under the seat in front of her and plopped down next to Hunter.

Kendall held her hand out toward the window seat on the other side of the aisle with only two seats.

"Would you like the window? After all, if it weren't for you and your peanut scare, we wouldn't have gone on strike, and we wouldn't be escaping to California. It's only fittin' that you should see it first."

"Thanks, Kendall." I scooted in to take my place by the window.

Kendall sat down next to me, unzipped her leather pack, and pulled out her burner phone.

"It's hard to believe that I actually forgot I had one of these. But I guess it can't do anything, so what's the use?" She flipped it open and looked at the screen. "Oh . . . whoops . . . I have eight missed calls!"

Heat popped to my cheeks.

"Uh-oh." I dug my phone out to check. Ten missed calls. And a couple of voicemails that I was afraid to listen to.

"I better call my mom." I pulled up the directory, where Papaw had programmed in "all the numbers we would need." I poked the one that said Maggie, and my heart started pumping a little harder.

The phone only rang once.

"Allie?"

"Hi, Mom." I leaned my head up against the window.

"Where are you? Your flight leaves in ten minutes."

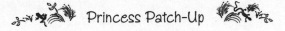

"I'm on the plane. We're all on the plane."

Mom sighed loud. "Oh, thank God. The guide said that you never showed up at the desk. What happened?"

"I'm not sure. We didn't see him, or we forgot, and we were hungry, and really excited . . ."

"Allie!"

"I'm sorry. What do you expect from a bunch of adolescents?" I kind of giggled, remembering how Austin squeaked out that term.

"I *expect* you to use the brains God gave you. Are you all okay?"

I examined my scratches.

"We had a little crash on the moving sidewalk, but no one lost any limbs."

"Allie!" Mom yelled into the phone again, and this time I had to pull it away from my ear.

"We're fine, Mom. Hey, I'm not supposed to be telling you anything about our trip! It's part of the agreement."

"Oops. Sorry, kiddo. But you were missing, and I'm your mom! I had to ask."

"Okay, but that's all the news you're gonna get from now on. How are you? How's the packing going?" I had to change the subject. Even if it was to *that*.

"It's awful. But one more closet is done. Hey, we met the new owners in person today."

"They aren't the owners yet," I said. "We've got a few more weeks."

"Okay, honey. I meant the *future* owners. They have a couple of kids your age. Twins—a boy and a girl. And get this—the man lived near Mamaw and Papaw when he was a kid, and he played with your dad and all your uncles. His name is Andrew Doonsberry."

"The Tablecloth Bandit?"

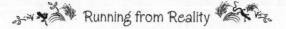

"One and the same. He still denies it, though. We had a good laugh about it this afternoon with him and his kids. I think they're going to make great neighbors."

At every family campfire since we've been little, our dads and uncles have told us the story of a demon alligator who lived in the haunted shed, and who one day long ago ate our Uncle Andy and a box of Mamaw's seasonal tablecloths. Since then, everyone had been scared to enter that shed—until Hunter's 'cousin initiation' last month—when we made him sit in there for an hour to prove the story was false. Then we learned, from Mamaw, that "Andy" was just a punk neighbor kid who stole Mamaw's tablecloths to make tents out of them, and our dads made up the story about the gator to scare him off.

And I guess it worked, for thirty years or so.

But now he's back. And he's stealing my house!

"So, is he still a punk?"

"No, Allie. He's been working as a lawyer in Florida for many years."

"Are his kids punks?"

"Allie!"

Kendall elbowed me. "Would you quit freaking your mom out? I'd like a little peace over here."

A voice came over the loudspeaker, and the plane backed up.

"Welcome, passengers. We will now begin our taxi out to the runway. We ask that you power down all electronic devices . . ."

"Mom, I gotta go."

"Okay, honey. I love you. Ryan and Brittany will meet you at baggage claim. Don't forget about them, silly."

I chuckled. "Maybe we will, maybe we won't."

"Allie-girl . . . you're impossible! But I love you, and I miss you already."

"I love you, too, Mom."

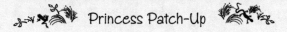

I flipped the phone closed and stuck it in an inner pocket of my backpack. In my shuffling, I brushed my hand against the lunch bag—which I planned to open just as soon as Kendall fell asleep.

CHAPTER 12

Bag of Wonders

"Peanuts or cookie?"

The flight attendant held out two packages.

Are you serious?

"No peanuts!" Kendall practically knocked the packets out of the flight attendant's hand. "This is Allie Carroway! If she eats a peanut in here, the pilot will have to land the plane in the ocean and we'll be calling the Coast Guard for a medi-vac."

The flight attendant's eyes widened. She pulled the peanuts away.

"Cookie, then?"

"Yes, I'll take the cookie, thank you. As long as it wasn't manufactured at a plant that also uses peanuts."

She examined the package. "I think you're good on this one." She handed it to me, gave me a polite grin, and went on to the next row.

"Kendall, that was a little dramatic, don't you think? Plus, I don't think we're flying over the ocean."

"Just looking out for my soon-to-be roomie." Kendall smirked. "I'm going to need you healthy to help me record some new songs I'm covering."

"Are you sure you have space in your room for me with all your musical stuff?"

"Well, I do have that extra bed. You might have to curl up in a ball, though, since my keyboard sits at the foot of it. But you're flexible, so that shouldn't be a problem, right?"

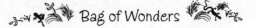

"Can I hang up my twinkle lights? I also have a mini-Christmas tree. If I give up foot space on the bed, can I exchange it for tree space in the corner?"

Kendall shook her head. "No, no, no! I'm not ready for Christmas. Plus, I can't write my melancholy songs with a bunch of cheery lights flickerin' in my head."

"Why do you have to write *melancholy* songs? And why aren't you ready for Christmas?"

Kendall rested her head back on her seat.

"I don't know why. Maybe it's because we already filmed Christmas—on Halloween."

"You're probably just tired." I pointed to the headphone jacks on the armrest. "After we take off, you should plug into some music and take a nap."

Kendall shrugged. "Sounds good to me. At least these seats tilt back."

"Yep. We're moving up in the world."

As we continued our never-ending taxi trip out to the runway, another flight attendant carried a little suitcase over to our row and reached up over Kendall's head to open the overhead compartment.

"Are you girls keeping your packs under your seats? If so, I'm going to put this up here. The compartments are a little crowded up front."

I was keeping my pack so I could peek into the Bag of Wonders.

"Sure, it's fine with us," I said, since Kendall had already plugged into the airplane music.

"Thank you. It belongs to one of those three men in row F, so if one of them comes over here during or after the flight to get it, don't be alarmed."

I gave her a thumbs-up. "Got it."

Hunter called over from across the aisle, "This is the longest taxi ride ever. I think we're driving to California."

It took us twenty minutes to taxi out and finally be cleared for take-off. Kendall still had her seat upright, but her eyes were closed. I prayed the jet roar and sudden g-forces wouldn't wake her up. That little brown bag in my backpack was burning a hole in my imagination. I couldn't wait to see what else was in there since Nathan told me it was *everything you need.*

The flight attendants rushed around, checking people's seatbelts and overhead compartments, but then finally settled down in their own seats facing us. They buckled their belts, and the one who had given me the cookie removed a mouthpiece from the wall and spoke into it.

"Flight 1145 is secured for take-off."

The jet turned, then stopped. Kendall stirred, the engines revved up, and the huge aluminum tube raced forward. I gripped my armrests and glanced over at my cousins on the other side of the aisle. Hunter had his cowboy hat back on, and he sounded like he was getting ready to rope a calf.

"I love taking off! Yee-haw!"

Soon the nose of the jet lifted, and the rising sensation tickled my stomach. I glanced out the window, and I realized why that guy Austin was so freaked out that we visited so many terminals. I could see them all now, and boy—were they huge and far apart. I spotted the little train that travels between them and laughed a little. Bigger than the island of Manhattan, for sure.

"Sorry we missed you, terminal D," I said, under my breath. "Maybe next time."

Kendall did wake up for a few minutes during takeoff. "Wake me if we go over the Grand Canyon," she said, and then she plugged back in and was snoring in seconds.

I dug into my backpack, trying to make the least amount

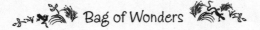

of noise possible. I felt around for the lunch bag, and gently moved it from my pack to my lap. I kept an eye on Kendall the whole time.

I pulled the in-flight magazine from behind the seat in front of me, and propped it up between my leg and Kendall's seat to use as a barrier. I stared at the crumpled bag in my lap.

Nathan, how did you know I would need Band-Aids?

My hands shook a little as I unfolded the top of the bag to pull out the next item—a headlamp.

"I already have too many of these," I said out loud, and then covered my mouth.

The headlamp was like the ten or so I already owned, and the two that I had packed in my backpack. The only difference was the camo. Instead of hunting camo—which blends into foliage in the bayou—this was "digital camo" which looked more like a desert blend.

I pushed the big button on the light a few times. With each push, it changed from a bright white light, to red, to blinking red. I fiddled with the strap, shortening and lengthening it with the plastic release clip. When I lengthened it, I spotted "Matt 51415" written in faded black ink on the inside of the strap.

Matt, huh? I thought your name was Nathan.

I reached in to pull out the next item—a folded-up map of the Hollywood Hills. When I opened it, a brochure for the Griffith Park Observatory fell out.

The next item was a gift card to In-N-Out Burger. Ryan and Brittany brag about going there all the time. In-N-Out was on our list of "things to do in Cali," but Ruby was especially inter-ested, and had been studying their "secret menu" for a week. Of course, if this gift card worked as well as Nathan's McDonald's gift card, it might not be so great.

I opened the bag wider and peeked inside. There was one

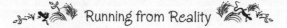
more thing—something that looked like a coin in the bottom. I put my hand in to grab it.

"Whatcha got there?"

I jumped, and the contents fell off my lap and scattered down around my feet.

"Kendall, you about gave me a heart attack!"

"Sorry! I woke up and noticed you checkin' out the mystery-boy bag, so I got excited. What's in there? Candy? Flowers? Engagement ring?"

"Very funny. It's just regular stuff. A light, a map, and a gift card for burgers."

"Oh." Kendall frowned. "Well, I guess that makes sense."

"Sense? Nothing about this makes sense to me."

"Allie, don't you see? He gave you the bag because it had a gift card in it." Kendall reached down to the floor and grabbed the card. She held it up. "He owed you money. Duh." Then she tossed it on my lap.

I shook my head.

"He said it had *everything* I need in it. He said that he was the last of his group to give his bag away. Kendall, I think this was a special project. Then he said I had kind eyes . . ."

"Sounds like he was payin' you back, gettin' rid of some junk, and flirting. Nothin' special."

Kendall wrapped up her earbuds and reached down to stick them in her backpack.

I spied the Ariel bandage on her leg and decided to blow her mind a little.

"Kendall, the princess Band-Aids were in the bag too."

Kendall stopped and looked up at me.

"What?"

"The box of Band-Aids came from the bag Nathan gave me. Kendall, the *exact* thing we all needed was the first thing

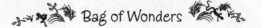

I pulled out of that bag! Plus, don't you think it's weird that they were *princess* bandages? You know it's my little inside joke with God."

Lately, I'd been grappling with the term "princess." My dad calls me that sometimes, and it bugs me, because I'm not really the frilly, tiara-wearing, live-in-a-castle-with-servants type. But recently, I've been thinking a lot about the fact that I'm God's girl, and since he's the King of Kings, that does make me a princess. I wear more camo than frills, but maybe God's idea of a princess is different than what's in the movies or printed on bandages.

Kendall focused on her Band-Aid for a minute. Then she turned her head toward me, and one side of her mouth turned up in a little grin. I think her one eye twinkled just a little too.

"Can I see the light and the map?"

I had her now. I reached down and retrieved the rest of the objects from the floor. I handed her the map.

"Hollywood Hills? Isn't that where all the movie stars live?"

I shrugged. "Maybe. And this fell out of the map." I showed her the brochure for the Griffith Park Observatory. On the front was a picture of a large white building, with three domes—the largest one in the middle—all situated on top of a hill that overlooked a large city.

"That could be Los Angeles," Kendall said.

"Do you think we're supposed to go there?" I fiddled a little with the strap from the headlamp.

"I vote yes." Kendall smoothed her hand over the front of the map. "Especially if it's near Hollywood."

I took the map and brochure back from her and gave her the headlamp. She inspected it, pushed the button just like I had, and then squinted to read the faded letters.

"Who's Matt?"

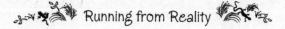

"Don't know. Maybe Nathan has a brother named Matt, and this is a hand-me-down. I have lots of passed-down equipment that says 'Ryan' and 'Cody' on it."

"I hear ya on that. Plus, you have a million of these, don't ya? I wonder why you 'need' this one?"

I shook my head. "I'm wondering about a *lot* of things right now."

CHAPTER 13

Wise Guys from the East

We flew for a couple more hours, and just when I felt like escaping from my window seat to do some cartwheels down the aisle, the captain's voice sounded over the loudspeaker.

"Ladies and gentlemen, we are beginning our descent into Los Angeles International Airport. Our flight attendants will be coming through the cabin to pick up any trash, and to make sure everything is secure. We should be landing in about twenty minutes, which will put us on the ground at five-thirty, Pacific Standard Time. The current temperature in LA is seventy-four degrees, so you can put those jackets away and enjoy the beautiful evening out there. Thanks for flying with us, folks, and we hope to see you soon on a return flight."

I snuck a look out the window at the twinkling lights of the city. "We missed the sun."

"We'll catch it tomorrow." Kendall pulled her seat upright and pushed her backpack under the seat in front of her. "We need to talk Ryan and Brittany into taking us to Hollywood."

"I wonder if it's anywhere near Santa Barbara? Hey, maybe we can take a picture by the Hollywood sign," I said, but then realized my mistake. No pictures on this trip.

"Yahoo! We made it to California!" Hunter took off his hat and waved it in the air like a cowboy riding a bucking bronco.

"Sir, please stow your hat or keep it on your head." The same flight attendant who tried to give me peanuts raised her eyebrows and motioned for Hunter to calm down.

"Whoops, sorry," Hunter said, and Kendall laughed a little. "Brothers."

"California, here I come!" Lola yelled. She's been waiting to say that for years. It had been her password to get into the Diva Duck Blind—back when we required passwords.

Landing in planes always unsettles me more than taking off, so for the next fifteen minutes my heart raced a little as I gathered my things, stowed them in my backpack, and shoved them under my seat. I gripped the seat arms and kept my eyes on the flight attendants who had buckled in for landing. Soon, I heard the wheels lower from the bottom of the plane, and a little after that they touched on the ground and the brakes took over. My body tried to pull forward, and I counted how many seconds it took to stop and reach taxi speed. About thirty.

I smiled. "Welcome to California," I said to Kendall.

The flight attendant spoke over the intercom.

"Welcome to Los Angeles, California. The time is five thirty-two. At this time, you may power up your electronic devices, but please remain buckled in your seats until we come to a complete stop. Be careful opening the overhead bins, as items may have shifted. Have a nice night, and we hope you choose our airline for your next flight."

Since we were in aisle twenty-two, we had to wait while couples with babies, elderly folks, and all the others in rows one through twenty-one retrieved all their carry-ons and moved forward. At one point, a stocky, dark-haired man started moving back toward us. He kept jumping into the seating areas of each row to let passengers by, and then he would jump out in the aisle again until he reached us.

He finally made it eye-to-eye with Kendall.

"How you doin'?" he asked in a booming voice.

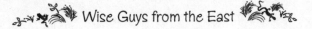

"I'm doin' good," Kendall boomed back, copying his accent, and then she looked at me with wide eyes.

The guy laughed and pointed at Kendall.

"Hey, that's a good accent! You from Jersey too?" What he said sounded more like "Joy-zee."

"Nah, she's just a singer-actor type of person," I said. "She's from the south, but speaks British, and apparently now she speaks Jersey. You must be here for your carry-on."

"Yeah, it didn't fit up there. You shoulda seen some of those women's handbags! It's like they got a whole boatload o'makeup stuffed up in there—ya know? Probably the kitchen sink too. I'm bein' rude. Name's Larry. I'm here with a couple of friends from my astronomy club."

Larry tipped his chin up at us and held out his hand to shake one of ours. Kendall shied away, but I stuck mine out.

"Nice to meet you, sir." I almost introduced myself, but then I remembered I was remaining anonymous, so I tried to fill the awkwardness with some other kind of conversation.

"New Jersey has astronomy clubs?"

"Yeah, they do. We like to look at the stars in the East, ya know? And—get this—we came here to LA to see the stars in the sky, not on the streets! I bet you don't hear that every day in Hollyweird."

"Allie, are you guys coming?" Lola yelled back at us from the front of the cabin. Hunter and Ruby were nowhere in sight.

"Sir, you need to move forward so the other passengers can de-plane." The flight attendant was behind us and trying to hold the swarm back.

Larry turned to look at the crowd. He hit his forehead with the heel of his hand.

"Oh—would ya look at that! I'm holdin' you all up. I just

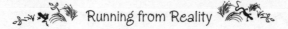

get busy talkin' and forget myself. I'll just grab my bag and get outta the way."

Larry opened the overhead compartment, and the carry-on suitcase fell out, knocked him in the chest, and landed on the ground.

"Sir! Are you all right?" The flight attendant tried to squeeze by to help him pick up the bag, but Larry put his hand out.

"I'm fine, ma'am, and I'm so sorry to cause such a ruckus." He reached down, picked up the suitcase, and pulled out the handle.

Then he waved to all of us behind him. "Enjoy your visits to California. If you get a chance, go see the *real* stars at the Griffith Park Observatory."

Then he turned and wheeled his bag out. It was pink and purple, with a sequined-silver star in the middle.

Kendall turned to me.

"Did he just say Griffith Park Observatory?"

Goosebumps popped out all over my arms.

"Yeah."

"That was weird," she said. "Who do you think that guy was?"

I shrugged. "You heard him. His name's Larry, and he's a wise guy from the East."

"I *gotta* take a picture of that suitcase," Kendall said, and she dug in her bag for her phone.

"Yeah, good luck with that," I said.

Kendall pulled out her burner phone, and scowled.

"PAPAW! You're *killin'* me!!!!"

CHAPTER 14

California Carroways

Ryan and Brittany found us on our way to baggage claim. "Sister intercepted!" Ryan put his arms out, wrapped them tight around me, and then lifted me and spun me around. When he put me down, he flicked my nose. "Welcome to Cali, Allie!"

"Dude, don't do that to your sister." Brittany came over and gave me a hug, then whispered in my ear. "You're brother's a menace. Let's ditch him and go shopping."

"Sounds good to me," I said. "But did you just call my brother dude?"

"She did," Ryan said. "Everyone and everything in California is called 'dude.' It cuts our vocabulary down significantly. I don't even have to learn my students' names."

Brittany brushed off the comment. "Don't you listen to that nonsense. He knows his students' names. And you'd be proud, Allie. He's been nominated for teacher of the year at his middle school."

My brother teaches eighth grade science. It's kind of a pre-chemistry thing. Not surprising, since he always loved blowing things up as a kid.

"That's cool, Ryan!" Hunter gave Ryan one of his warm hugs, and all the other cousins lined up to greet the California Carroways.

"We came as far as we could into the airport without having to go through security," Brittany said. "We heard you had a little problem getting lost in Dallas."

"We were never lost," I said. "We were on an adventure in terminal hopping."

Ryan laughed. "Well, you don't want to terminal hop in LAX. This place is a nightmare. Come on, let's go get your luggage."

We followed Ryan and Brittany down a few hallways packed with musty-smelling people until we came to the carousel that promised to deliver the bags from flight 1145 from Dallas-Fort Worth. We waited about fifteen minutes before the belt started moving.

"Are you guys hungry?" Ryan asked.

"Oh, please, can we go to In-N-Out?" Ruby asked. "I've been dying to order the animal-style fries."

"But we just had fries at the Cowboy Chow Down," Lola said.

"Those were Texas fries," Ruby said. "California fries are different."

Ryan rubbed his belly. "I'm always up for In-N-Out."

We grabbed our bags as they plopped out on the conveyor, and soon we were on our way out to the parking garage.

"How far is Santa Barbara from here?" I asked Brittany, as I hoisted my suitcase into the back of a red minivan.

"Two-and-a-half hours," Brittany said.

"Really? That's far!"

"California is huge," Brittany said. "But don't worry—we're not going to Santa Barbara." She wiggled her eyebrows up and down.

"What?" I scratched my head. "Isn't that where you guys live?"

"Not this week. Surprise!" Ryan jumped and put both arms up in the air. "We're goin' to Hollywood, baby!"

The goosebumps on my arms returned.

Ryan dug in his jeans pocket, and pulled out some keys.

"I have here a set of keys to a five-story mansion located in the Hollywood Hills, that once belonged to a famous

mother-daughter acting team—Abigail and Gabriella Fremont. Abby and Gabby. People called them the 'Gabi-girls.' You're too young to remember them—but they were quite famous and made tons of movies together."

"And how did you end up with those keys?" I crossed my arms and narrowed my eyes.

Brittany laughed. "Oh, you know your brother. He meets people, charms them, and then they give him stuff."

It's true. Ryan is one of 'those' people. He loves to chat with complete strangers everywhere he goes. He has a great smile, a sweet baby-face, and he's easy-going and funny. People love him, and it's not just because he's on TV. People have been giving Ryan things for years. When he was a kid, he was always getting invited to go places with his friends. Disneyland, Hawaii, the movies, skiing, camping, you name it.

"We just love that Ryan," everyone would say.

I don't blame them. I would never say it to his face—because he's my brother—but he's pretty much my favorite person.

I zipped open my backpack, reached into the 'Bag of Wonders,' produced the Griffith Park Observatory brochure, and handed it to him.

"Is this anywhere near where we're staying?" I asked.

Ryan's eyes nearly bugged out of his head.

"Yes! And this is my *favorite* place! Do you want to go there? Please, say yes! I can show you the giant periodic table, and the planetarium, and the Foucault Pendulum! It's gonna be great!"

Brittany shook her head. "You're such a science nerd."

"Yes, I am." Ryan handed me back the brochure. "Well, are we just gonna stand here or are we going to go and fight the LA traffic?"

Hunter punched his fist in the air. "Fight, fight, fight, fight, fight!"

Ryan walked around to the side of the minivan, pushed a button on his keychain, and the door slid open.

"Cool, huh? This belongs to one of my students' parents who's a car dealer. He had a bunch of extra vehicles sitting around, so when I told him I was going to be chaperoning you guys for a week, he offered to let me use it for free."

"Of course he did," I said.

We piled in. Lola, Ruby, and Kendall took the back seat, and Hunter and I settled in the two captain's chairs in the second row.

"This is plush," Hunter said. "And check out the swivel." He turned his seat around to face the girls behind him.

Ryan started up the van and backed out of the parking space. "Well, I hope you're comfortable. Hollywood is only thirty miles away, but I wasn't kidding about the LA traffic. We could be in here all night. In-N-Out is only a half-mile away, so we can get fueled up for the trip. I feel like I could eat a four-by-four tonight!"

"Are y'all talkin' about a truck?" Kendall asked.

"That's four meat patties and four pieces of cheese," Ruby whispered. "Shh. It's a secret."

We pulled into the In-N-Out parking lot in minutes.

"Order anything you want, it's on me," I said as we piled out of the van, and I waved my gift card in the air.

"We need hats," Ryan said.

"Aren't we a little old for that?" Kendall asked.

"Aw, come on, Kendall. Where's you tourist's heart?" Ryan opened the door and yelled into the restaurant. "Bayou kids, comin' through! First time at In-N-Out!"

People looked up and waved, but then went back to eating their grub.

"Ryan," I said, "we're trying to be anonymous so we can enjoy ourselves."

"Oh, that's right. This is the big 'Run from Reality' tour. Well, I'm tellin' you right now, sis, reality has a way of finding you wherever you are, so you better learn to enjoy it—whatever it is."

Right now, reality was burgers and fries.

"Let's all order off the secret menu," Ruby pulled some crumpled-up notes out of her jeans pocket and scanned them.

"I've never even ordered off the *real* menu," Lola said as she stepped up to the counter. "I'll take a burger, fries, and a chocolate shake."

"Allie, try the grilled cheese," Ruby said.

"Okay. "I'll take a . . ." I cupped my hands around my mouth and whispered to the girl taking our order. "Grilled cheese." I spoke the rest of my order at regular volume. "And I'll have a strawberry shake, and some fries with that."

"I want a burger, fries, and a drink—all animal-style," Hunter said.

The girl laughed. "Drinks just come regular, since the animal-style includes mustard."

"Oh, good call," Hunter said.

It was Ruby's turn to order. She wrung her hands and finally spoke. "I've been thinking about this for a long time, and here's what I'd like: A grilled cheese, animal-style fries, and a root beer float."

"And we'd all like hats, please," Ryan said, and then he pointed to me. "And she's paying. But she's not famous or any-thing, so just take her money and don't ask for autographs."

The girl winked. "Gotcha."

She took Ryan's and Brittany's order, which did include the famous four-by-four, and then I gave her my gift card, which had enough money on it to pay for everything.

Thanks, Nathan.

She handed the card back to me. "You have twenty-five dollars left. Thanks for choosing In-N-Out."

You better believe I was happy to choose In-N-Out. The next thirty minutes was a taste sensation—fries, secret sauce, grilled onions, and gooey cheese—my favorites.

"Hey—check this out! It's my favorite verse!" Ruby held her root beer float cup up and pointed to some red letters on the bottom. "Proverbs 3:5."

"What? Let me see that." I reached for the cup.

"I have one too," Lola held up her Coke. "John 3:16."

"They have Bible verses printed on most of their wrappers," Brittany said. "I hope people go home and look them up."

"I have Revelation 3:20 on my burger," Hunter said. "No wonder it tastes like Heaven."

We all giggled, chewed, gulped, and wore hats like tourists. And to my surprise, no one in the whole place came over to ask for an autograph or selfie with the famous Carroway family. It was the best meal out ever.

When we were clearing our table and taking our trash out, Kendall pulled me aside.

"Allie, do you think Matt 51415 could be a Bible verse? Like from the book of Matthew?"

There was something in her face that lit up when she said that. I decided to give her a hard time.

"Kendall, if that were true, then that would make the head-lamp special in some way, and I thought you said that the stuff in the bag was nothing special." I threw my trash in the bin, and then brushed my hands together.

"Well, maybe I was wrong. After all, we did need the princess Band-Aids."

"And the gift card," I added.

"Okay, *and* the gift card. So maybe we should get a Bible

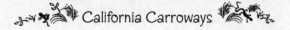

out and check out some verses. I'd check my Bible phone app, but my phone is with *Papaw*."

She was cracking me up the way she kept saying *Papaw*. Kind of with a growl.

"We can look it up later tonight. But don't get too excited, Kendall. Remember, it's just a dumb old, not-special bag, which was given to me by a broke-and-flirty, not-special-at-all, surfer-boy—who, by the way, happened to use the word "dude," so he could live in California."

"He really said 'dude'?"

"Yes. He did."

"Well, then, that's somethin'."

"I definitely think so."

CHAPTER 15

Movie Star House

It took us two-and-a half hours, through road construction and three major traffic snarls, to finally travel the thirty miles to our destination in the Hollywood Hills. It was dark, so we couldn't see much, except narrow roads that curved—first up, then down. Somehow, we finally made it to Star Drive, which was the street where the Gabi-girls' house was located.

"Here it is, I think," Ryan said. "It's 51415 Star Drive." He pointed to the stone wall that had glowing numbers sticking out from it.

Brittany squinted out the window.

"All I can see is a wall and a garage. Where do you suppose the rest of the house is?"

"Look up, my dear," Ryan said. "You gotta look up."

He pulled the van over to the curb and we all climbed out. Then we all looked up.

"It's too dark to see anything," Hunter said.

"Hang on, I have a light." I opened my backpack and pulled out my bayou camo headlamp, and poked the button to turn it on. Nothing happened.

"Is it broken, sis?"

I shook the headlamp and then tried the button again.

"Hmmm. Batteries must be dead. But hey, no worries—I got another one."

I pulled the pink one with the duck pattern out of another pocket, and I poked.

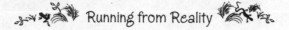

Nothing.

Kendall grabbed both headlamps out of my hands.

"Are you kiddin' me? These are both dead?" She shook them around and poked and poked.

"What kind of bayou kids are you—not havin' lights?" Ryan chuckled.

"Hey, you're from the bayou too, you know. And as a matter of fact, I do have another one."

I reached in my pack again, and I worked my hand into the Bag of Wonders. I felt for the fabric strap, and pulled out the digital camo headlamp. I held it up, looked over at Kendall, and winked, then pushed the button.

The blazing stream of light illuminated the off-white house, that looked like it was built right into the hill. Curved tiles covered the roofs, and switchback stairways lead back and forth up to the porches and balconies that jutted out from each level. Vines of some kind wound their way around the sides of the house, and bright flowers hung over the wrought-iron handrails that lined the walkways.

"Wow." Lola's head tipped back as far as it could go. "Are we really staying here?"

"Ryan, where did you say you got these keys?" Brittany moved over and wrapped her arms around Ryan's waist.

"Uh, one of my student's parents is a descendent of the Gabi-girls, and the owner of this house. The tenants moved out a few months ago, so it's been vacant, and they wanted someone to stay during Thanksgiving week to guard against the . . ."

"Guard against what?" Lola's head snapped back.

Ryan waved his hand. "Ah, it's nothin'."

"Ryan, tell us!" Brittany shoved Ryan to the side.

"Nah, I'm not gonna tell you, because it's not a big deal. They just want it to look like someone lives here so the

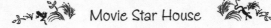

Hollywood Hoodlum doesn't show up and vandalize the place. Oops, I told you."

Kendall gasped. "Hollywood Hoodlum?"

Ryan laughed. "His nickname is the 'Hollywoodlum.' He sounds scary, but he's just some punk who's been going around, breaking into vacant homes, and destroying all the beautiful old furniture and memorabilia. Don't worry. He's no match for folks from the bayou. Hunter could take him down with a roll of duct tape."

"Wait," I said. "You know about that incident with the gator?"

"Sis, we all do. You can't hide anything from the folks."

"Ryan, are you *sure* this is safe?" Brittany pushed her long, blonde hair behind one ear. "Mom and Dad are trusting us with the kids."

"It's gonna be fine, because we'll be *in* the house. That's the idea. Make it look like someone's here. And in this case, we've got a lot of *someones*. Now, would you people like to see inside a movie star's home, or not?"

"I totally want to check it out!" Hunter lifted the gate on the back of the minivan, pulled out his suitcase, and ran up the walkway over the garage to the first level. We all followed, lifting our rolling suitcases whenever the ramp gave way to a few stairs.

"This must be the main entrance," Ryan said. "Allie, hold your light over the keyhole." I did, and Ryan inserted the long, old-fashioned key into the old-fashioned keyhole—the kind people look through in mystery movies to spy on people. Ryan turned the key, and we heard a loud click. He opened the tall wooden door, and it creaked.

"Sounds like it needs a little WD-40." Ryan felt around for a light switch, and we all bunched around the entrance until he found it. We stepped inside.

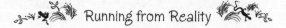

"Wow." Lola just couldn't find new words today.

"Stunning." Brittany put her hands on her hips and looked up.

"Magnificent." Kendall took in a breath and grabbed her throat.

"It's bright, that's for sure," Hunter said.

We all stared at the same thing—a humongous crystal chandelier that hung in the circular entryway. It seemed like it held at least a hundred electric candles, and from each candle, dozens of crystals hung, reflecting the light all over the walls of the room.

"I could lay down and sleep right here and be happy," Ruby said.

"Hey, look!" Hunter pointed to a wall hanging at the side of the room. It was a message, written in black calligraphy, framed in a gold frame.

Let your light shine before men so they will see your good deeds and praise your Father in Heaven.

"Were the Gabi-girls Christians?" I asked.

Ryan shrugged. "Don't know. We'll have to Google it."

Kendall sighed. "As if any of us has that capability."

"Let's check out the rest of the place," Ryan said. "I think they said this house has twelve bedrooms and seven baths."

"Are you serious? We can each have our own bathroom?" Lola ran her fingers through her hair. "I won't have to fight for mirror time?"

"We can almost each have our own level," Ryan said. "I'll take the bottom, so I can fight off the Hollywoodlum when he comes in. Unless of course, he swings in from the top on vines like Tarzan. Hunter, you should take the top level so you can catch him and wrap him up with your tape."

"Cool!" Hunter said.

"Ryan . . ." Brittany shoved him again.

Ryan laughed. "I'm sorry, I can't help myself."

We continued to be amazed by every room at each level of the house. The Gabi-girls must have loved light, because there was a chandelier in every room—not quite as huge as the first one. And each one gave its room a warm, golden glow.

Light-colored wood floors were covered by thick throw-rugs in every room. Kendall and I chose to share a room with a white cushy rug that covered the whole floor, an extra-tall bed with a white quilt, and two tan wingback chairs. White lace curtains hung from the ceiling to the floor, and opened to reveal a glass sliding door leading to a large balcony overlooking the city.

"I see why they built up the hill now," Kendall said. "This view makes climbin' all those stairs worth it."

We stared out at the lights that flickered all over.

"It's beautiful," I said. "Hey, look, Kendall!" I pointed right. "There's a Christmas tree! Isn't is magical? Won't it be great to have one in our room at home?"

Kendall rolled her eyes, but I could tell I was wearing her down.

"It's nice," she said.

And then I remembered something.

"Speaking of magical, we gotta check and see if that headlamp has a Bible verse on it!"

Kendall's mouth dropped open. "Oh, yeah! And now we know that you needed that headlamp too. Who would have thought you'd bring two headlamps with dead batteries?"

"I know!" I ran back in the bedroom, pulled my suitcase up on the bed, and unzipped it. My Bible sat right on top of everything. I grabbed it and headed for a wingback chair. Kendall followed.

"Okay, Matt 51415. We'll start by looking in Matthew.

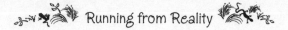

What chapter? Five? Fifty-one? No, I'm pretty sure there's no fifty-one."

Kendall knelt next to me. "Try chapter five, verse one."

I flipped through till I came to the worn pages in Matthew. I've read that book a lot.

"Here it is. Matthew 5:1: "*One day as he saw the crowds gathering, Jesus went up on the mountainside and sat down.*"

"Hmm," Kendall said. "We're kinda sittin' on a mountainside right now."

I shook my head.

"I'm gonna keep looking. How about . . . Matthew 5:14?"

I took my finger and moved it from the bottom of the page to the top.

"How about this? Matthew 5:14: "*You are the light of the world, like a city on a hilltop that cannot be hidden.*"

"Whoa. Kendall, I think this is it! This verse is on a headlamp—and it's about *light*."

Kendall crowded in closer to my Bible.

"It says 51415. Maybe you should read verse fifteen too."

"Okay, here goes. '*No one lights a lamp and then puts it under a basket. Instead, a light is placed on a stand, where it gives light to everyone in the house.*'"

"Wow, that's just like this house."

"Allie!" Kendall just about blew out my eardrum. She poked her finger in my Bible. "Read the next verse!"

"Matthew 5:16: "*In the same way, let your light shine before men so they will see your good deeds and praise your Father in Heaven.*

I dropped the Bible in my lap. "That's the verse in the frame downstairs. Kendall—this house, and this headlamp, have some kind of connection. And now—for some reason, I'm part of it too."

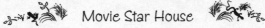

Kendall gasped and jumped to her feet. "And that's not all!" She ran over to the bed, snatched the headlamp, then grabbed my hand and pulled me down the three levels of the house, out to the entryway, past the bright chandelier, down the dark walkway, until we were at garage level.

"Why are we outside? Do you want to run into the Hollywoodlum?" I huffed and puffed, and looked both ways.

"No." Kendall pointed to the stone wall.

"Shine your light on the wall. Check out the address. I just realized what Ryan said it was."

I poked the button, pointed it toward the wall, and the light reflected off the white stones.

51415 Star Drive.

CHAPTER 16

Sleepless on Star Drive

For most of the night, I lay awake, staring at the starlight out the slider door and trying to figure out what in the world was going on.

This is just a vacation, right, God? Are you trying to tell me something? I know I wanted to run from reality, so are you playing a trick on me, letting me run into something totally unreal?

"Allie, are you awake?" Kendall lay on her back, and her arms were out of the covers. Her hands were folded on her stomach.

"Yeah. I can't sleep."

"Me either. My cuts are throbbing."

I smoothed my hand over one of the bandages on my forearm.

"Was that just today when we piled up on the moving sidewalk?"

"Yeah. It seems like a long time ago. I wish we had a video of that."

"It was kind of hilarious."

"Yeah."

"I miss my phone with all the music on it. I usually fall asleep listening to songs."

"Oh. I guess you'll have to settle for the crickets."

"I guess."

Kendall hit the bed. "It's so quiet! How do you normally fall asleep?"

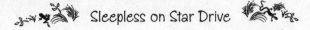

"Me?" I had to think about that for a minute. "I mostly fall asleep talking to God."

Kendall turned on her side and looked at me.

"Really?"

"Well, either talking or listening. I guess I'm kinda rude, because I fall asleep in the middle of our conversations all the time."

"God's probably okay with that."

"Yeah."

Kendall returned to her back. "Okay, I'm gonna try it."

"Try what?"

"Having a conversation with God. It's been a while."

"Really?"

"Yeah."

"Then I'm sure he misses you."

"We'll see."

Silence.

"Good night, Allie. I'm glad we're gonna share a room soon."

I smiled. "Me too. Good night, Kendall."

Kendall fidgeted for a little while, but then I could hear her breathing even out, so I knew she had fallen asleep.

But I couldn't. I kept going over the entire day in my mind. Starting with Nathan and his azure blue eyes.

Who are you, kid? And what's with your bag?

CHAPTER 17

Hair and Hills

I woke the next morning to Kendall singing in the bathroom. And then a little yell.

"Oh, I love being a redhead!"

I sat up and rubbed the sleep out of my eyes.

"Allie, come in here. I need your honest opinion."

Oh, boy, this was going to be interesting. Everyone knows not to ask me for an honest opinion if they don't really want it.

I put on my slippers and padded into the attached bathroom. I rounded the corner, and had to rub my eyes again.

"You look like a poinsettia," I said.

"Don't you just love it?" Kendall raked her fingers through her shoulder-length, now red hair.

"It's . . . *bright* red," I said.

"I know. That's the point. People will look at my hair and not my face, so they won't recognize me as Kendall Carroway. Ta-da!"

"But what if they see you from a distance and think, 'Hey, is that hair, or is that girl wearing a Santa hat,' and then they come closer and realize it's you?"

Kendall kept flipping her bright hair while looking in the mirror.

"Well, I doubt that will happen, but if it does I have these!" Kendall ran to her suitcase in the bedroom and brought back a pair of large round sunglasses. "And for this trip, I'm goin' choker-less!"

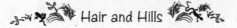

I grabbed my neck. "Wait a minute." I shuffled closer and looked right in her eyes. "Are you really Kendall? Or are you . . . the . . . Hollywoodlum?"

Kendall threw one of her chokers at me. "Maybe *you* should wear one. I don't see you comin' up with a disguise, and you're the most recognized Carroway."

"I brought a couple of ball caps. I'll stuff my hair in them and pull the bill down over my eyes."

"And people will think *you're* the Hollywoodlum."

"Hey, in there! Anyone awake? Turquoise streak comin' through!"

Lola charged into the bathroom, with Ruby not far behind.

Lola looked stunning with that short dark hair of hers that lays perfectly around her head.

"I think I like the turquoise even better than the pink," she said. Then she frowned. "Too bad Hannah won't let me keep it."

"You get to keep it for this week," Kendall said.

"You look amazing," Lola said to Kendall.

"I thought so." Kendall fluffed her hair and stuck her tongue out at me.

"Have you looked outside?" Ruby asked. "It's beautiful. The hills are covered with greenery and bright fall flowers. I say we go on a hike."

"I'm up for that," I said. "I wonder how far it is to the Hollywood sign?" I walked back to the side of the bed where I had stashed my backpack with the Bag of Wonders in it. I pulled out the map of Hollywood Hills and spread it on the round, gold coffee table that sat between the two wingback chairs in front of the bed.

"When did you get this?" Lola asked.

"Yesterday," I said, and I shifted my glance toward Kendall.

Ruby put her finger on the map and followed one of the lines with it. "Is this the way?"

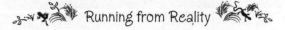

"Nope. Those are streets. The trails are much thinner lines. Let's find Star Drive and then we can figure out what's up."

I checked the map index and got the coordinates on the map for Star Drive. Then I positioned two fingers on the letter and number, and pulled my fingers in to touch each other on the map.

"Here we are. Star Drive."

Lola put her finger on the map.

"And here's the Hollywood sign. Looks like there are a few ways to get there."

"Well, let's go get Ryan, Brittany, and Hunter and see if they want to go check it out."

Ryan, Brittany, and Hunter were just returning from a trip to the market, and each carried two bags into the massive kitchen area.

"Oh, look, the Hollywood beauties have finally awakened!" Ryan reached into a canvas shopping bag and produced a box of bakery items. "Would you like some orange juice and scones?"

"I feel spoiled," Ruby said, and she lifted a mini blueberry scone to her mouth, took a bite, and closed her eyes. "Yum."

"What would you all like to do this morning?" Brittany asked.

"We would like to hike to the Hollywood sign," I said.

Ryan reached his hand out to give me a high-five.

"Let's do it! Meet out on the curb in fifteen minutes!"

We scarfed the scones and juice, then went to our rooms to put on long pants, sweatshirts, and jackets. I put my hair in a ponytail, pushed it through the back of my ball cap, and pulled it down so my eyes were hidden.

Once outside, we knew we had all made a mistake.

"It's *hot* out here!" the redheaded Kendall exclaimed.

Ryan and Brittany—who were dressed in tank tops and shorts, just laughed at us.

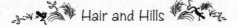

"Yeah, you're gonna want to change," Brittany said. "It doesn't get cold around here until . . . um . . . it doesn't get cold around here."

"I didn't bring shorts," I said. "Did anybody bring shorts? Well, besides Hunter."

Hunter stood there smiling in his long black basketball shorts.

"Go change into the coolest things you have and we'll go shopping later," Ryan said, and then he shook his head. "Bayou kids. And don't forget a water bottle. We're going to be climbing."

We were back in ten minutes in T-shirts, capri pants, and carrying water bottles we found in the refrigerator. My head was sweating inside my hat, and now I wondered if I should have picked a hair dye color for myself instead of a hat disguise.

"Okay, troops," Ryan clapped his hands together. "Do you want to do the short hike to the Hollywood sign or the long hike to the Doowylloh sign?"

"Huh?" I scrunched up my nose.

"The long hike goes above and behind the Hollywood sign," Brittany explained. "You can see more of the city, but then you see Hollywood backwards, which spells Doowylloh. It's about a mile longer."

"I vote short and Hollywood," Kendall said. "We'll still get a good view, right?"

"Absolutely," Ryan said. "Let's get this show on the road."

I was sweating a lot before we even got up the first hill.

Kendall caught up to me and whispered in my ear. "I wonder why your special bag didn't come with a pair of shorts?" Then she giggled.

That reminded me that there was one more thing in that bag that I hadn't checked out yet.

We huffed and puffed while our feet stirred up dust on

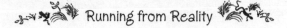

the dirt paths. Runners passed us, and we passed families out walking their dogs with their children. We went by a horse stable, and some people riding horses, which now added the unpleasant task of watching every step so that it didn't land in a horse pile. When it seemed like we had hiked two miles, we came to a sign, signifying that we were on the Mulholland Trail.

Brittany pointed out our options on the sign.

"Only .7 miles to go to the view by the water tank. That should get us close enough for a picture."

"No pictures, remember?" Ruby said. "We made a deal with Papaw."

"Then we'll have to capture it in our memories." Ryan pointed to his head.

"I feel like we've already gone five miles." Lola sighed as her arms drooped down to her knees.

"That's because you aren't used to climbing mountains," Brittany said. "Allie, how's your breathing?"

I breathed in deep and let it out.

"It's great. I wonder why?"

"It's a little drier here in California. Not a mold spore in sight during this drought." Ryan stopped and pointed to a steep trail that veered off the path and up the mountain that looked like it bypassed at least three switchbacks. "Anyone up for a shortcut?"

"Ryan, don't go up there." Brittany shook her head and kept walking.

I stopped and assessed the climb. A couple of guys and a kid were almost to the top.

"I'll go," I said. "I'm a slimy mess anyway. It looks like fun."

Everyone else backed away.

"Oh, come on, people. Where's your sense of adventure? I bet the Hollywood sign is right up there."

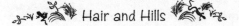

"I'd go," Hunter said, "but I don't want to lose my cowboy hat."

"It looks too steep. I don't want to take a chance on any of you getting hurt." Brittany—who is a third-grade teacher—is paid to be sensible.

"We're already cut up," I said, and I pointed to my princess bandages. "Ryan, how about just you and I go?"

Ryan's eyes lit up. "Okay, sis, you go first, and I'll catch you if you slide. This is going to be fun." Then he turned to the rest of the group. "We'll be kicking back waiting for when you arrive."

Brittany put her hands on her hips. "You make me crazy, Ryan Carroway. Be careful!"

Ryan and I jumped off the main trail and looked up to the top of the steep hill.

"We can do this Allie-Cat. It's not even as long as a football field."

I took my first steps up the cracked, brown hillside. Dry brush lined the thin trail that had been worn by other adventurers before us. About a third of the way up, my foot slipped and I landed on my right knee.

"Oww."

"Time to get on all fours," Ryan said, and even he was puffing a bit now. "Think like a lizard. Stay stuck to the hillside and you'll be fine."

For the next third of the climb I kept my belly off the ground. But the last third—no chance. I had to pull with my hands, push my feet up on a few jutting-out rocks, and slither like a snake. I choked a little when I inhaled some brown dirt that swirled in the breeze.

"You can do it, Allie! We're almost there!"

I felt a river of sweat trickle down my back, and I looked up to see a chain-link fence at the top of the hill.

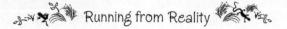

"Ryan, we have a little problem. We have to climb a fence!"

"Uh . . . okay . . . just keep going. We'll figure it out when we get there."

I slipped on some loose gravel and kicked Ryan in the head. "Oops, sorry."

"No problem, squirt. I'm having the time of my life!"

I think he really was. And I had to admit, it was fun hanging out with my big brother all by myself.

"Just a couple more steps. We can do this!"

Ryan grabbed my foot and pushed it up. That's just what I needed to make it to the top. I gave a little "whoop" when I saw that there was a little opening to the side of the fence that we could squeeze through.

"We did it!" Ryan gave me a sweaty high five as we rejoined the "official" trail to the Hollywood sign.

I gasped and pointed to his forehead.

"You're bleeding!"

Ryan reached up and dabbed his finger on the wound.

"Dude, you've always kicked hard."

"I'm sorry. Hey, I have a princess bandage for you." I reached in my backpack and pulled out a Cinderella. "Here you go."

"Thanks." Ryan peeled the bandage out of its wrapper and slapped it on his head. Then he pushed me toward the edge like he was going to throw me back down the hill. I squealed, and he stopped, of course. "Good adventure, Allie-gator."

"Best thing about it was there were no cameras," I said. "Just me and you having fun without the world knowing about it." I reached down and knocked some dirt off my pants, and then brushed my hands together.

"Really? I think it would have been great to have the film crew here for that. Don't you think it would make people laugh

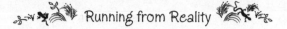

to see you kick me in the head? I think our show brings a lot of people joy."

"Okay, now you're sounding like Papaw." I punched him in the arm. "Stop it."

Ryan stretched and looked around at our new surroundings. "There's a sign. Let's go find out where we are."

We approached the short wooden sign with carved white letters.

"Hmmm," Ryan said, and he put his hand to his chin. "We're overachievers. Seems we may have climbed too high. The water tank trail is down the hill. I think everyone else is going the other way."

"What? I didn't climb all the way up here just to walk back down. What's up the hill from here?"

Ryan pointed to the sign. "The back of the Hollywood sign is just .5 miles away."

"Cool. Let's go there."

Ryan reached over and brushed some dirt off my cheek. "You never go along with the crowd, do you?"

"Only if the crowd is going the best way." I smiled and turned up the trail. Ryan followed. "I'll call Brit and tell her not to expect us."

A few switchbacks later, we landed at the back of the Hollywood sign.

"Wow! You can see everything from here! Is that downtown Los Angeles? Is that the *ocean*?"

Ryan laughed. "Yeah, it is. We're lucky to be here on a clear day."

"Uh-oh." I frowned. "The ocean looks navy blue. Lola will be disappointed it's not turquoise."

"It's hard to tell from here, goofball," Ryan said. "Plus, it looks different all the time. Sometimes it appears green,

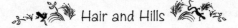

turquoise, navy, mud brown . . . depends on the elements. Would you like me to explain those to you?"

"No." I pulled the bill of my cap up a little. "Where's the observatory?"

Ryan pointed to the left. "Over there. It's mostly covered by the mountains. You can see the domes. Wanna walk over there? I think it's eight miles."

"Sounds like it would be a nice drive, then." I spied a little bench on the trail. "Right now, I would like to sit here and try to burn this view into my memory, since I'm not allowed to take pictures."

"Sounds good to me." Ryan let me sit, and he walked around, back and forth, between the D and the H, in Hollywood, marveling at the view.

"Hello." A voice attached to a little girl wearing light pink shorts and a gray T-shirt approached me on the bench. "Do you have any Band-Aids?"

The question made me smile.

Yes, but I'm running out. Everyone is bleeding on this trip.

The little girl had a bloody knee, but you wouldn't have known by her face, which was grinning ear-to-ear, revealing two missing front teeth.

"That's a nasty scrape," I said. "You came to the right person, because I have a box of princess Band-Aids here in my backpack."

Her eyes got big. "Can I borrow one?"

I patted the bench seat next to me for her to join me.

"You don't have to borrow it, I'll give it to you."

The girl sat down.

"Thanks!"

I looked around. "Are you here by yourself?"

She shook her head.

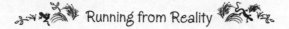

"No. My daddy is over . . . there."

Her dad was in a conversation with Ryan, and the two were already laughing. Soon he'd probably give Ryan the keys to a limo or something.

I opened the backpack and pulled the bandage box out of the bag.

"Pick a princess," I said, and I handed the box to her. She searched for a minute, and then pulled out Ariel.

"Good choice. My cousin has her same hair color, only redder," I said, and then I laughed a little.

The girl opened the bandage package and started to pull the tabs off the back.

"Hang on," I said. "Let's clean it a little." I pulled my water bottle out of the netted pocket on my pack, opened it, and poured some on her knee. Then she used the bottom of her T-shirt to wipe it off.

"Thanks. I shoulda worn long pants."

"No, shorts were a good choice. It's blazing out here."

The little girl pushed some of her long, wavy light-brown hair behind her ear.

"Do you got an extra pony?"

"I sure do." I reached into the side pocket of my backpack and produced a stretchy band. Then I helped gather her hair up in a high ponytail.

"Look!" She pointed to my ponytail. "Just like yours, but I don't got a hat. My neck feels cooler. My name is Angela, what's yours?"

I cleared my throat. "Um . . . it's Allie."

"Nice to meet ya, Allie."

"Nice to meet you too. So, what brings you to . . . uh . . . Doowylloh?" I pointed to the back of the sign. "Do you live here in the hills?"

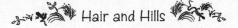

"No. Do you?" Angela swung her legs forward and backward.

"No. But I'm staying in someone's beautiful house. Are you on vacation?"

She kept swinging. "No."

"Hmmm. Are you on a day trip?"

Angela nodded. "A couple of days. We're waiting for a miracle."

I turned my head to look at her, but she was just grinning, looking out at the city.

"What kind of miracle?" I asked.

"The only kind there is—from God."

"Oh." I nodded. "I get you."

"And I hope he hurries up, because my mom is having a baby."

"Right now?"

"No!" She laughed. "On Thanksgiving."

"Well, that sounds exciting!"

She shook her head. "Not if we don't get the miracle."

"Is there something I can do?"

"Nope." She crossed her arms. "Only God does miracles."

"You have a lot of faith. How old are you?"

"Seven. Is that old enough to have faith?"

"Of course." I glanced back at the steep trail that brought us up here. "Did you walk all the way up here?"

"Yeah. I have lots of energy. Daddy wanted me to get rid of it."

"Well, this hike should do it."

"I think so."

"Angela, are you ready?" Angela's dad walked halfway over to us. "We can run all the way down the hill if you want."

Angela slid off the bench. "Sure!" Then she turned back to me. "It was nice meeting you, Allie. Thanks for the Band-Aid and the ponytail."

"You're welcome. And I'll be praying about your miracle and your baby."

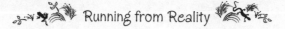

"Thanks!" Then she turned and began running with her dad down the hill.

"Allie, do you want to run down the hill?" Ryan laughed and approached the bench.

"No, but I *am* ready to get out of this California sun for a while. Are you sure it's November?"

I gathered up the bandage box and pulled out the Bag of Wonders to store it. As I opened the bag, I heard something shift in the bottom. Oh, yeah—there was one more item in there!

I reached in . . . and pulled out a small key.

We found the rest of our crew halfway down the hill.

"Allie, you missed being in the Hollywood sign picture with us," Kendall said. "Oh, wait—no, we didn't get a picture because of . . . *Papaw.*" Then she growled.

"Hey, you need to stop blaming Papaw," Ryan said. "He just gave you what you wanted. And don't forget that he sent you to California for free."

"That *was* cool," I said.

"So, do you guys want to go to Malibu today?" Ryan has endless energy—like my new friend Angela. "Allie's concerned about the ocean color."

"Not after that fifty-mile-hike," Kendall said. "Can't we just go back to the house and veg?"

"Yeah," Lola said. "I want to be fresh and rested when we go to the beach."

"Well, we could go back and swim in the pool," Brittany said.

"Wait . . . there's a *pool*? People, why are we standing around talking?" asked Hunter.

CHAPTER 18

Dumbwaiter Discovery

Houses in the Hollywood Hills are huge, and they wind around the hills in funny ways. At least this one did. That's why I hadn't discovered the pool and fabulous patio that existed behind the left side of the house.

"This is unbelievable," I said to my cousins, as we all lay around on lounge chairs after a refreshing swim. (At least I did remember to bring a swimsuit.) "Did just the Gabi-girls live here in this huge house?"

Brittany picked up her phone. "I don't know. I'll Google it." She poked the screen, and in seconds came up with the answer.

"It says here that Abigail married her high school sweetheart, Reginald Fremont, in 1932. He believed his wife had the prettiest face in the world, with a beautiful voice and acting ability to boot, so they moved to Hollywood, and he worked odd jobs day and night to support her so she could prepare for and audition for anything that came up."

"That's so sweet," Lola said. "I'd like to marry someone like that."

Brittany continued. "Soon, Abigail was discovered by the famous movie producer, Theodore Wallace."

"Wallace Films?" Hunter said. "They make tons of movies!"

"Yes." Brittany kept reading. "Abigail's movies were so popular that she helped propel Wallace Studios to the giant they are today. Let's see . . . it says here that in 1936, she gave birth to a girl, Gabriella Marie Fremont, and . . ."

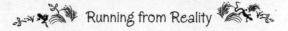

Brittany frowned and stopped reading.

"What?" I sat up on my lounge.

"Two years later, Reginald died in a car accident on the Hollywood freeway."

"NO! That's not a fairytale ending!" Lola covered her face with her hands.

Brittany continued. "Abigail was devastated, but determined to raise her daughter to love the industry that her husband worked so hard to support. She gave her dance, voice, and piano lessons, and she took her along on all her movie sets. The backstage crews helped raise Gabi—which is what she liked to be called—and as soon as there was a movie part that suited a little girl, Mr. Wallace cast her in it. The rest is history. The Gabi-girls starred in a total of thirty-two movies together, between 1946 and 1960, and each had a stellar career on their own too. Abigail had this house built in 1950, and she made sure there were lots of rooms so they could invite friends and relatives to visit. The women were especially close to Reginald's many sisters. It says he had five."

"Did Gabi ever get married?" Kendall was full into the conversation now.

"Hang on." Brittany scrolled down on her screen. "Yes, it says here that she was married briefly to a guy named Wilson Greyhound, and they had a son named . . . Gabriel. Oh, dear . . ."

"Briefly?" Lola looked like she was going to cry. "Did Wilson die too?"

"No. It says that one day Wilson disappeared, never to be heard from again. And on the day he disappeared, he withdrew several thousand dollars from Gabi's savings account."

"He stole her money?" Hunter took off his cowboy hat and put it over his heart.

Brittany nodded. "Gabi was heartbroken. She never tried

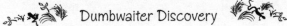

to find Wilson, and she changed her son's last name from Greyhound to Fremont."

"That's a horrible story," I said.

Brittany grinned as she scrolled some more.

"Well, here's a bright spot. It says here that Abi and Gabi were Christians, so they raised Gabriel together in this house and took him to church every Sunday. He grew up, got married, and became a minister at a church in Santa Barbara. He and his wife have four boys and one girl, ages thirty all the way down to eight."

"So Gabi got to be a Mamaw! That makes me feel better." Ruby smiled.

"It says here that Abi died in 2007, and Gabi died in 2011. That's the end of this article. If you want to know more, you'll have to do more than Google." Brittany put down the phone and sighed. "Looks like God blessed a lot of people through those two ladies—despite their hardships."

Lola looked like she wiped a tear from the corner of her eye. "I wish they were here so we could talk to them. Especially Gabi—to find out what it was like to be a kid star back then. I wonder if they ever made her wear a camo beanie."

"I doubt it," Kendall said. "This is California. But I bet she got zits from time to time."

"Now I want to go explore the house, and find out more," I said.

"Me too!" Hunter said. "I bet the room I'm staying in was Gabriel's."

"I don't know how much you'll find out," Ryan said. "It's pretty much bare bones—just furniture and wall hangings left in here. Even the bookshelves in the library are empty. If you really want to know more, I'll see what I can do. Gabriel's son is in my class at school. They were the ones who let us use the house this week."

"I want to see *all* the rooms." I stood up and threw on my swimsuit cover. "Maybe they left some family photos somewhere."

"Let's explore and meet in the kitchen to share what we find in one hour." Ryan took Hunter with him, Lola and Ruby teamed up, and that left me and Kendall to go together.

Brittany put her floppy hat over her eyes and laid back down on the lounge.

"I'll just hang out here and keep the pool safe from the Hollywoodlum."

"I need a snack or somethin' first," Kendall said. "Swimmin' makes me hungry. Let's go find some grub."

I followed Kendall into the kitchen, and as she pulled out the goodies, I looked through cupboards for any kind of clue to the history of the Gabi-girls.

"Hey, what is this?" The wall next to the pantry had a cut-out with a secret compartment of some kind. It looked like just another cupboard, but when I opened it, it revealed a big box with ropes hanging next to it. I pulled down on the ropes a little, and the box moved up!

"Kendall, check this out! It's like an elevator for cats or tiny dogs."

Kendall came over in a flash. "Hey, that's a dumbwaiter! I see them in British movies all the time."

"A dumbwaiter? What does that mean?"

"Well . . ." Kendall put on her British accent. "It's like this, my dear. Sometimes objects are simply too heavy or awkward for the servants to carry. For instance, if you were taking afternoon

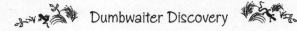

tea and sandwiches to an upstairs sitting room, you would place them in this dumbwaiter, pull the ropes, and everything would be safely delivered, without losing a drop."

"We need one of these in my new house. I hate carrying things upstairs."

"Shall we try it out? Let's get some snacks, shall we?"

Kendall went back to the counter and piled some fruit, crackers, and cheese on a platter.

"We'll try some lemonade too. Might as well be adventurous."

Once we had the box all filled, I pulled the rope, and our food disappeared . . . upward.

"When do I stop pulling? And how do we know where to go to find our stuff?"

Kendall looked up the tiny elevator shaft. "I think it should stop at some point. Keep pulling till you feel resistance and then we'll go find the other opening upstairs."

"This is fun," I said, and I pulled till it stopped.

"I bet I find it before you!" Kendall took off out of the kitchen. But I'm faster than her, so I caught her on the stairs.

We both stopped on the second floor and dared each other go down the hall. But then we tore up another flight. The dumbwaiter had to go higher than that.

Kendall took off down the hallway on the third floor, but I went up to the last level. I knew there was a rooftop patio up there. And that would be the place to have afternoon tea.

I also discovered a laundry room. And . . . bam! The dumbwaiter was up on this floor too.

I ran over to it—it looked just like the cupboard in the kitchen—and I opened the door.

"Hmmm." I stared inside the dumbwaiter. It appeared that I hadn't pulled the rope quite far enough. The box with our food was only halfway there. I poked my head in the shaft, and then

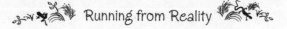

reached my hands in to see if there was a way to lift the box up a little more. I grabbed for anything I could find and felt a flat rectangular object on top of the shelf. I pulled it out.

It was a thin book with purple flowers all over it. No title, and it had a strap with a lock on the side.

"Allie! Did you find it?"

I hid the book behind my back.

Kendall rounded the corner, breathing hard. She stopped in front of me and stared me down.

"Ugh! You always beat me! Just once I'd like to beat you— hey, what do you have behind your back?"

She reached around me, but I pulled it the other way.

"I found it on top of the dumbwaiter. I think it's a diary."

"You think? Open it up!"

I shook my head. "I can't. It's locked."

"Then it *is* a diary! I wonder whose it is?"

Kendall reached for the book, but I pulled it away.

"You don't have a key, do you?" Kendall put her hands on her hips.

"Well, of course not. Do you?"

I shifted my eyes to the ceiling.

"Allie, why are you acting so funny? Did you find a key in the dumbwaiter? Aww, come on! Quit messing with me!"

"Come with me," I said, and I led Kendall back to our room.

"When I was on the hike, I found one more thing at the bottom of the Bag of Wonders." I walked over to my side of the bed and lifted my backpack off the floor. I unzipped it, pulled out the bag, and fished out the little key with pink plastic molding at the top of it.

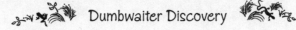

Kendall put her hands on her cheeks.

"Do you think it will fit this diary?" I asked. "That would be the craziest thing in the world if it did."

Kendall thought a moment. "Allie, those little keys open bunches of things."

"But why is it in *this* bag, that also had a map of the Hollywood Hills in it, and we happen to be in the Hollywood Hills, not to mention that we have a headlamp with the address of *this very house*?"

Kendall jumped up and down a couple of times.

"What are you waiting for? Try to open it!"

My hands shook a little as I settled the book on the bed and tried to line up the teeny little key with the teeny little lock. I pressed it in, and jiggled it. First left, then right. Then I yanked on the strap to see if the little hooks would disengage.

"Nothing," I said.

Kendall frowned. "Try again. My diary at home is picky about how you twist. Give it a little quicker wrist action." Kendall tried to show me, with an action that looked like she was dangling a treat for a puppy.

"Okay, here goes." I dangled.

And then we heard a click.

I pulled on the strap, and the lock opened.

Kendall stuck her head right next to mine as I opened the flowered book. The first few pages stuck to the cover, and I had to pry them down to see what was written inside:

Diary of Gabriella Marie Fremont.
November, 1948

"Wow." Kendall's eyes were wide.

I carried the book over to the wingback chairs, like I was

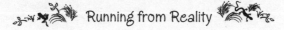

carrying a delicate platter filled with china tea cups. I let myself down gently, and slowly turned the page.

"You're gonna to read it to me, right?" Kendall was in the other chair, leaning forward though—so she was barely sitting in it.

I nodded and began:

> Today is my birthday. Momma gifted me this diary and encouraged me to write down my thoughts, dreams, plans, and prayers. That I will do, but I will also share my frustrations, since I cannot express them to the masses —or they would think me selfish and unsophisticated —which is exactly what I am.

"I like this girl already," I said.
"Go on!" Kendall was staring laser eyes through me.

> I once dreamed of joining my mother on the big screen. But now I would like to take that dream back. I didn't know it would require so much tap-dancing! I pray the day will soon arrive when tap-dancing will no longer be appreciated, and I can give up the rat-a-tat-tat that hammers in my brain each day when I walk on the set.

"Huh," I said. "Tap dancers always look so happy. I wonder if they all feel this way?"

"Keep reading!"

"That's all she wrote about that." I turned the page and continued to read:

I hate sleeping in curlers. How is one supposed to rest one's head on a pillow when one's head is wrapped up in rigid plastic? I pray the day will soon arrive when curly hair is no longer appreciated, and I can once again feel the softness of down next to my cheek at night.

"I feel her pain," I said.

"Yeah," Kendall said. "Go on."

I turned the page, scanned the next entry, and giggled. "Allie! Read!"

Thoughts about makeup. It was invented for my stylist, Laura, to torture me. The fake eyelashes feel like spiders, and the lipstick tastes like plastic and makes my lips stick together (must be why it's called lipstick!). I pray for the day when makeup is no longer appreciated and I can be a regular naked-lipped girl, and sip lemonade through straws without turning them a blazing red color.

"This is hysterical! Gabi sounds like a Hannah."
I turned the page.

Learning lines is a bear. What do writers know about a twelve-year-old's vocabulary? Most of the time, it is necessary to keep a dictionary in my dressing room, to discover what I am saying in a script!

"Well," I said, "at least with reality TV, they let us talk like we talk."

"Yep, we got that goin' for us, y'all."

I rested my back against the chair and looked up at the ceiling.

"Allie, I wonder if all child stars wish they weren't stars sometimes?"

"I wonder if Gabi ever wanted to dye her hair Santa Suit red?"

"Probably. She sounds spunky."

"Kendall! Allie! Come quick! We found a secret dance room!" Lola's voice echoed through the hallway, and for some reason I jumped up off the chair and hid the diary under my pillow on the bed.

"We'll read more later," I told Kendall. "For now, let's go see Gabi's tap-dance chamber."

CHAPTER 19

Star Calling

We explored the Gabi-girls' house for a little while, and then swam again, in the ninety-degree weather.

We barbequed hamburgers for dinner, and made S'mores for dessert, which we ate while sitting on the patio at the top of the house, looking out at the city lights.

"Malibu tomorrow?" Lola asked.

Hunter scrunched his nose. "I was hoping to go to the tar pits."

"Tar pits! Sounds like it was named after a boy's underarms," Ruby said. "I don't think I wanna go there."

"I agree," Lola said. "Plus, it's a sad, sad, story Hunter. Trust me. You'd rather go play beach volleyball with us."

Hunter hung his head. "But you know I want to be a paleontologist. Why would I come this close to the tar pits and not go visit?"

Ryan came to his rescue. "I have an idea. How about the boys go check out the pits and the girls go to the beach? You can shop a little on the way there and back too. And Hunter and I will shop for tacos—not clothes." Ryan patted Hunter on the back.

"I vote yes!" Hunter said. "I already have all the clothes I need, but I have been lacking tacos."

"Okay, then. Tar and Tacos it is." Ryan gave Hunter a high-five.

Kendall and I laughed till we cried as we read some more excerpts from Gabi's diary that night.

I would venture to say that sequins are the most ridiculous clothing adornment.

Caviar is disgusting. I smile, and put it in my mouth to be polite, but then I spit it out in my milk.

Today on the set, we discussed how to hide my newest pimple — which is right on the end of my nose. I suggested using a sequin, but Laura did not find that funny.

"I knew it!" Kendall said. "Zits span the decades."

Today, someone slid an autograph book under the stall where I was "resting" in the women's bathroom at Macy's, but they didn't offer me a pen. I sat there for ten minutes, not knowing what to do, until a hand reached back under and stole the book away.

"That girl's a hoot!" Kendall said. "She should have written a book."

I held up the diary. "Ahem. She did."

"Well, I'm glad. I really needed a good laugh." Kendall stretched and yawned. "That swimming and hiking killed me

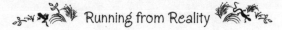

today. I better go to sleep if I'm going to play this silly beach volleyball that Lola's all fired up about tomorrow."

Kendall spent a few minutes in the bathroom and then came out and dove under the covers. She turned out the light, but I wasn't ready to sleep just yet. I pulled the "Matt 51415" headlamp out of my bag, turned it on, fastened it on my head, and threw a blanket over myself on the chair so I could read more.

After Kendall was sound asleep, I found exactly what I needed:

January 1, 1949

The valuable thing about diaries is that you can go back and read what you've written and see how ridiculous you were a few days prior. I have noticed in my writings a pattern of complaining, and I am disturbed by it.

Today, being that it is the first day of a new year, I have determined to complain less. I read this in my Bible this morning:

Rejoice always; pray without ceasing; in everything give thanks: for this is the will of God in Christ Jesus to you. 1 Thessalonians 5:16 (ASV)

I regret that I have not been rejoicing or giving thanks in all my situations —

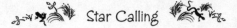

especially for my life on the movie set.
Today I received a letter from a little girl
who has a club foot, and she wrote that
when she watches me dance, it brings her
joy. That caused me to think deeply about
my life, and to wonder:

Lord, have you called me into this life
of stardom for a reason? Do you have a
bigger plan for all this tap-dancing?

I paused, and put the book down on my lap.

Lord, have I been complaining a lot?

I didn't really have to listen for God's answer, because I already knew it. The answer was yes.

I turned off the headlamp, and sat in silence under the blanket for a few minutes.

I'm sorry, God. Show me how to stop complaining about my life.

I waited a little longer, and right about the time I started to break a sweat under the blanket, I heard a still, small voice deep down—somewhere in the middle of my soul. It said, *"Focus on me, not on you."*

"What?" I said that out loud, and then remembered that my blanket was not soundproof.

Anyone who tries to hold onto his life will lose it, and anyone who loses his life will find it.

Okay, that had been a memory verse for me a while back. And I didn't quite get the meaning, until I heard the next thing.

"Allie, your life is not about you."

CHAPTER 20

Sand and Tar

The next morning, we all piled into the minivan and drove Ryan and Hunter to the rent-a-car place so they could pick up a Mustang convertible for the drive to the La Brea Tar Pits.

"Don't wear your cowboy hat with the top down," Lola said.

"And leave the bones there!" Kendall waved and Hunter flashed his famous smile as they drove away for their tar and taco adventure.

We girls picked up some deli sandwiches and other snacks at the grocery store, and then headed out through the beautiful Malibu canyon on our way to Lola's dream beach.

It didn't disappoint. Except that Lola's hair streak didn't exactly match the water. Today the ocean was a rich, azure blue.

"It's spectacular!" Lola threw her arms out to both sides—like she would hug the ocean if she could. "Smell that salty air! Who wants to go swimming?"

The answer was—all of us. We threw our tote bags and backpacks on the sand and ran out to immerse ourselves in the warm . . .

"It's freezing! Aaaack! What? Why is it so c-c-cold?" Ruby wrapped her arms around herself and jumped up and down in the ankle-deep water. Kendall shook her head and ran back to her towel and wrapped up. Lola and I tried to be brave. After all, you don't get in the Pacific Ocean much when you're from Louisiana.

And now, with all the goosebumps that were appearing all over my body, I was thinking that's a good thing.

"I need to go wrap up in a blanket too," Lola said.

"No. We came all this way. Let's go *all in*." I stepped out a little deeper, and a wave came and splashed up to my waist.

"Brrrr. Are you sure, Allie? All those surfers out there have wetsuits on." She pointed out at a cluster of people sitting on boards in the distance.

I nodded. "That's because they're sissies. We can survive a few minutes in here, no problem. I dare you to dunk that turquoise streak under the water."

Lola scowled at me. "Allie, you're nuts!"

"Do it!" I yelled, and when the next wave came in, I ran toward it and dove into the surf.

I was numb in seconds. When the water receded and I stood, Lola was next to me, drenched from head to toe.

"Makes you feel fully alive, doesn't it?" I shivered in the breeze.

Lola pointed at the surfers.

"T-t-they are not sissies, they're smart."

Another wave came and splashed us up to our shoulders. I shivered some more.

"Okay, maybe you're right. Let's go find our towels. We've completed our mission and conquered the mighty Pacific."

It was like a race back to find our towels. Ruby saw us coming and held one out for Lola and wrapped her up in it.

"What a nice sister," I said. I looked around. "Anyone seen my towel?" I searched through my tote and the surrounding area for the yellow thing with the big orange butterfly on it, but it was nowhere to be seen.

Brittany looked around.

"I haven't seen it, Allie. Are you sure you brought it?"

I stood there, freezing water dripping down my body.

"Uh . . . maybe I didn't bring it. Maybe I left it at the pool."

Just as I said that, the sun went behind a cloud.

"I also may have forgotten to bring a sweatshirt."

"I'm sorry," Brittany said. "I should have warned you that California beaches can be cold." She pulled a towel out of her tote bag and swung it around me.

I shivered a little bit more. "That's not what you see in the movies," I said. "And it was so hot yesterday."

"That was inland," Brittany said. "It's probably hot there now too. It should warm up here for a couple of hours before the fog rolls in this afternoon. Make sure you put on sunscreen. The sun can burn you even though you feel like you're freezing."

I sat down, wrapped in the towel, facing the waves, and watching the surfers.

"How does anyone stay in there long enough to learn how to do that?"

"It's amazing the difference a wetsuit makes," Brittany said.

"Allie," Ruby said, "your lips are turning blue."

"Oh, dear." Brittany came over and knelt next to me. "Are you breathing okay? Did you bring your inhaler?"

I gestured over to my backpack. "Of course. I never forget that. I only forget unimportant things, like clothes. But actually, my breathing is fine."

Lola pointed down the beach. "Is that a shop over there? Maybe they sell sweatshirts."

"I bet it is," Brittany said. "Let's dry off and go shop. If we're going to stay here for a while, Allie's going to need some warm clothes."

"Sound good to me," I said.

"Yeah," Lola added. "We can't leave until we play volleyball and until I sketch a sunset for Papaw."

The little shop was called "The Malibu Hut," and it had sand piled inside on the floor. I had my choice of lots of souvenir

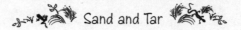

sweatshirts, hats, flip-flops, and more. I picked out the warm-est sweatshirt I could find. It was a soft, light-gray hoodie, with the word *Malibu* scrawled in scribble letters across the front. Shells were sketched below the letters, with a swoosh of orange, pink, and yellow sunset colors sandwiched in between. I bought sweatpants too.

"Ryan's going to give you a hard time, you know, after all that talking about needing to buy shorts." Brittany paid the cashier for my clothes, and at the register, she threw in a pair of socks and a ball cap to match.

"You didn't have to do that," I said. "I have money saved."

Brittany winked. "Papaw sent me some money. You can thank him."

The shopkeeper let me use the fitting room to put my new clothes on over my suit. When I finally emerged, my cousins were chomping at the bit to get out of there.

"Okay, can we go play some volleyball now? I got my souve-nir." Lola batted around a turquoise volleyball that said "Malibu Beach" on it. The ball matched the streak in her hair.

"Let's go!" I said. And just as I did, I spotted a familiar sandy blonde surfer wearing a *Surf & Son Summer* T-shirt run-ning past the open door of the Malibu Hut.

I watched for a second, not knowing what to do.

Could that be him?

"I'll be right back!" I yelled, and I ran out of the hut.

I looked left and right. No surf heads to be found. Then I spotted him—at least I thought it was him, getting into the back seat of a green Jeep, which backed up and rolled out of the parking lot, and into Malibu Canyon.

"Allie!" Brittany chased me down, like I was a toddler get-ting ready to run into the street. "Your parents will never speak to me again if I lose you. What were you chasing?"

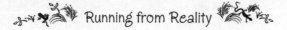

I watched the cars zooming in the distance.

"Reality, I think."

"Oh." Brittany shaded her eyes and looked in the same direction as me. "Well, that's progress. Come on, let's go smack a volleyball around." She put her arm around my shoulder and turned me back toward the beach. "That should warm you up."

"Okay, who are the teams?" I jumped over on the side of the net that I liked the best. "Should we go by age or by athletic ability?"

"What are you tryin' to say?" Kendall stood at the back of the sand court, straddling the line.

"She's trying to say that some people, though they might be the oldest, are not volleyball players," Lola said. "But I appreciate your showing up to make my dream come true."

"I don't think sisters should be on the same team either," Ruby said. "We might fight."

"Well, that means . . ." Lola gave Kendall a funny look.

"That I'm on your team! Aren't you lucky today?" Kendall smiled and jumped over on Lola's side. "Don't worry—I'll let you hog the ball all you want."

I whispered to Ruby, "This will be short and sweet. Just keep hitting it to Kendall."

"I heard that!" Kendall yelled. "You are not very nice to take advantage of a less athletic cousin. If you don't treat me nice, I will refuse to sing at all your weddings!"

I scooted to the back of the court and got ready to serve.

"Zero-zero!" I tossed the ball up with my left hand and hit the ball overhand with my right. It zoomed over the net, heading for Kendall, just as I had planned.

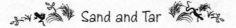

Kendall, however, side-stepped out of there, and Lola came diving in to dig the ball up and over the net, taking Ruby and me both by surprise. We sorta just stood there while the ball hit the sand.

"Good one, Lola! Our team rocks!" Kendall clapped and put her thumbs in her ears and flapped her fingers at us. "Take that—athletic cousins!"

Lola served next—a rocket that tipped the top of the net and then dropped in between me and Ruby. Two-zero.

The next five serves were a bunch of aces by Lola. Ruby and I jumped left and right, back and forth, but we never got a single body part to touch the turquoise fire bomb.

"Girls. Here's a tip. You have to fling yourself in the sand," Lola said.

"But I'll get sand in my clothes," Ruby said.

I laughed. "You get muddy all the time at home. What's the difference?"

"Sand gets in your teeth and your ears and your eyes and your nose and, well . . . everywhere else. I get the feeling that the sand I take home today will stay with me forever."

We won the next point, because Lola couldn't stop laughing at Ruby's sand explanation, so she served the ball into the net.

"Thanks for the break," I said. "Kendall, this one's comin' for you!"

"I'm ready!" Kendall yelled, and she stood all the way at the back of the court, so Lola could have all the space she would need to dive and destroy us.

Brittany stood outside the court, acting as our referee, and laughing.

"I'm getting hot now," I said, and I started to peel off all the new clothes I had just bought. Soon I was back to my swimsuit.

And I tried to dive, which worked. But Ruby was right. Sand was everywhere, and a ton of it stuck to my sweaty legs.

"This is not my favorite sport," I said. "We're only playing one game, right?"

Lola even tried to brush sand off herself between serves. "It's fun, but it's not as glamorous as it looks on TV, and it's a lot dirtier than playing in the gym. I might just stick to that."

A few minutes later, Lola and her invisible partner Kendall had wiped the court up with me and Ruby.

"Anyone want to take a dip in the ocean and clean off?" I asked.

"NO!" was the response from every single person.

Instead, we found a water spigot near the parking lot, and we tried to wash off as much sand as possible. But the truth is, Ruby was right. Most of that sand was coming back with us, probably all the way to Louisiana.

"What time is sunset?" Lola asked.

Brittany checked her phone. "4:45," she said. "Let's go for a walk, get some ice cream, and then sit on our towels and wait for it."

That's what we did. And it was worth the wait.

"Don't tell Papaw, but not taking pictures is causing me to pay attention to things better." Lola sat on her towel with some colored pencils and her sketch pad in her lap.

"Me too," Kendall said. "And I keep forgetting to check my phone. Has anyone gotten a call from home?"

We all shrugged. "I didn't even bring my phone with me," I said. "It's not like I don't want to call anyone. I'm just not thinking about it."

"Papaw says that when he was a kid he just played outside all day and nobody knew where he was till he came in for supper."

"That wouldn't be so bad," Ruby said.

Kendall laid back on her towel. "Do you think anyone on this trip has recognized any of us?"

I shook my head. "I've been keeping an eye out. No one has taken a secret picture, no whispering, no staring. It's kinda weird. I wonder if anyone in California even watches our show."

"Well, if they don't, they should," Kendall said. "It's funny, informational, and uplifting."

"Really?" I said. "And this is the same show you want to go on strike from?"

Kendall was quiet for a minute. "Maybe it's not so bad after all."

"Oh!" Lola said. "I wish I could have recorded what you said just now."

"Yeah, well, you'll just have to keep it in your memory vault."

The sunset hit its most beautiful point—with reds and oranges and yellows all mashed together to look like a heavenly smoothie.

"You guys, I feel like saying a prayer," Brittany said. "Is that okay with you?"

"Sure," Ruby said.

We all bowed our heads, and Brittany began:

"Lord, I want to thank you for this beautiful day that I got to spend with these beautiful girls. Help them to always turn to you for everything in their lives, and help us all remember that we are your shining lights in the world. In Jesus' name, amen.

And just as we raised our heads, we watched the sun slip below the horizon. And in a funny way, I actually wished the film crew could have been there.

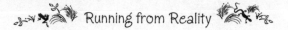

We met Ryan and Hunter at In-N-Out for dinner after our separate adventures.

"The poor dinosaurs. They got stuck in the tar, and it took them months to sink. There are tons of bones in those pits." Hunter hung his head and looked like he was going to cry.

"Isn't that a paleontologist's dream?" I asked. "To find a million bones all in one place?"

Ryan gave me a tense look and shook his head, and then he drew a finger across his throat to signal me to change the subject.

I put my hand on Hunter's shoulder. "Hey, guess what. We found out that the Pacific Ocean is freezing cold, and that beach volleyball players are really sand monsters."

Hunter smiled a little. "We had some good tacos."

I smiled too. "And we saw an awesome sunset."

"I kinda miss home," Lola said. "I wonder what our parents are doing?"

"Duh, people. Remember—it's duck hunting season. How soon we forget."

Kendall laughed. "It doesn't seem like such a big deal from way over here in California."

"Because there are no leaves and no rakes," Hunter said.

"That was the point of the vacation," Ryan said. "To give you some perspective."

"When do we go to the Griffith Park Observatory?" I asked. "I hear you can get a great perspective on everything from there."

"Monday," Ryan said. That will be the best day for seeing the moon at its finest."

"I can't wait," I said.

CHAPTER 21

Hollywoodlum?

The moon was close to full as we drove back to the Gabi-girls' house after leaving In-N-Out. As we approached the driveway and Brittany got out to open the old-fashioned double-door garage, we spotted a person running down the stairway leading up to the front door.

"Who was that?" Ruby yelled, and she pointed to the back of a young man running up the street. He had what looked like a baseball bat resting on his shoulder.

"Uh-oh," Ryan said. "That doesn't look good."

"Was it the Hollywoodlum?" Hunter asked, and he slid open the side door of the minivan and started to run in the direction of our intruder.

"Hunter, come back here!' Ryan yelled, and Hunter stopped and turned.

"He might be dangerous," Brittany said. Then she glanced up toward the front door. "Ryan, do you think anyone else is up there?"

"I'll go take a look. You kids stay put."

Hunter jumped back into the van and we all waited while Ryan climbed up the stairs. It was about five minutes before he returned.

"Coast is clear. I checked most of the bottom floor. There's evidence of someone trying to pry the door open and also a big dent in the door."

Lola gasped. "Do you think it was the Hollywoodlum?"

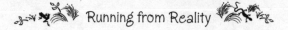

"Could be," Ryan said. "Maybe he thought the place was deserted. See, it's a good thing we're housesitting!"

Brittany sat in the front seat of the van and crossed her arms. "I'm not so sure it's a good thing now. We could be in trouble if he comes back."

Ryan brushed off her comment. "Nonsense. Did you see that skinny kid? Hunter could tape him to the wall with his duct tape. Plus, we scared him off. I'll call the police and let them know what's going on."

Ryan let us out of the van and pulled it into the garage. Then we all walked up the staircase to the front door, and saw the door damage for ourselves.

"I'm glad he didn't get in," I said. "He could have destroyed the chandelier."

"Maybe we should turn on all the inside and outside lights, so he can tell that someone's home," Lola said.

"That's a great idea," Brittany said.

"But what if he does come back? Shouldn't we have a plan?" Hunter paced from the beat up front door back to the top of the stairs leading up to the entryway. He looked up, side-to-side, and then over the fencing toward the street. "We could come up with a battle plan."

"That won't be necessary," Ryan said. "I doubt that kid will be back. He might not even be the Hollywoodlum. Maybe he was just selling something."

"Like baseball bats?" Brittany asked. "When did you last encounter a door-to-door baseball bat salesman?"

A few minutes later, a policeman came walking up the staircase to the front door.

"Are you Ryan Carroway?" the policeman asked, and Ryan stepped forward.

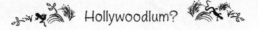

"That's me,' Ryan said, and he reached out to shake the policeman's hand.

"You look like a guy I've seen on TV in the bayou." The officer smiled. "My family loves your show. It's the only time we all get together during the week, with all our busy schedules. It's nice to have something positive to watch together."

It felt good to hear that.

"We're glad you like it," Ryan said. "Man, you got here fast."

"I was patrolling just a block away when you called in. Mind if I ask you a few questions for the police report?"

The officer pulled out a notepad and pen from his back pocket.

"Not at all," Ryan said. "Let's go out by the pool and talk. I'm gonna let these kids go up to their rooms and get ready for bed."

We took our cue and streamed up to our rooms on the top floors. Kendall and I arm wrestled to see who would get the first chance at the shower. Kendall won. That girl can be athletic when she wants to.

I was happy because it gave me a chance to sneak a peek into Gabi's diary while I waited. I pulled it out from under my pillow and flew over to the wingback chair and opened it. The next entry was disturbing.

Last week, a reporter inquired as to what things I love the most in life. I told him Jesus, my mom, reading, tulips, hot fudge sundaes, and puppies. Today, the interview appeared in the Hollywood Sun. He left Jesus off the list!

"That's not right," I said, out loud.

"What's not right?" Ruby poked her head in the door. I closed the diary and pushed it behind the throw pillow.

"Just reacting to something in my book. Did Lola beat you to the shower?"

Ruby skipped over to the other chair. "Always."

She looked around. "Every room in this house in magical." She wrapped her arms around herself. "I get such a warm, comfortable feeling here. I think it's all the light."

I smiled. "Me, too. I wish I could take pictures to show my mom and dad."

"Maybe Ryan can get this place again and we can all come out for a vacation next time."

A knock came at the door, only it was open. Hunter had knocked on the doorpost.

"Permission to enter?" Hunter stood there, wearing a new green La Brea Tar Pits T-shirt with his long basketball shorts. The shirt said "Save the Dinosaurs."

I grinned and pointed to the shirt. "Nice. It's too late, you know."

"I know." Hunter plopped down cross-legged on the floor next to our chairs. "But it's not too late to save this house from the Hollywoodlum!"

He had a sneaky little gleam in his eye, so I had a feeling we were in for a little project.

And I wasn't wrong.

CHAPTER 22

A Star in the West

Our day to visit the Griffith Park Observatory finally arrived. I think I was more excited to go there than if we were going to Disneyland, since the place was connected somehow to Mystery Boy Nathan's Bag of Wonders. We waited to go later in the afternoon, so we could hang around and see the moon and stars over the Los Angeles night sky. All day long, I experienced butterflies in my stomach and random goosebump outbreaks as I waited to finally pile in the van.

Ryan pulled the minivan into the parking lot of the Observatory.

"We have two choices. We could ride the shuttle, which takes forever to get here, or we can climb the hill." Ryan pointed up toward some steep switchbacks, and I could just see the tip-top of one of the domes of the Observatory in the sky.

"I have one word," Kendall said. "Shuttle."

When we were in the middle of the hike up—all huffing and puffing, Kendall spoke again.

"Did anyone hear me say, 'shuttle' earlier? Because I'm pretty sure I said 'shuttle'."

Ryan got behind Kendall and began pushing her up the hill.

"Just a few more steps, girl. It will be worth it."

About a thousand steps later, we saw it. The Griffith Park Observatory sat in the distance behind a grassy area with a fountain in the middle. Kids ran in circles, playing on the lawn, as adults rested on folding chairs eating snacks, and enjoying the afternoon California sunshine, which now that we weren't at the beach, seemed a little too hot.

"Hope it's cooler inside," I said.

"Oh, it's the coolest ever, dudes. Wait till you see the life-sized periodic table."

Ryan increased his stride.

Brittany picked up the pace with a slow jog to keep up. "Your brother's a science nerd, and he's not even ashamed."

Hunter grinned. "I want to be a science nerd!" Then he picked up the pace too.

We all reached the front entrance to the Observatory about the same time, except for Kendall. She strolled happily, humming to herself as she brought up the rear.

"Okay, I don't expect us all to stay together like a school field trip, but don't leave the building, and stay with a buddy. Papaw added me as a contact on your burner phones, so call me if you can't find us. There are some shows starting in a little while, so we can get tickets to those if you're interested."

Ryan held out his arm and motioned for me to lead the way. "Prepare to be amazed."

We entered a circular room, with people everywhere and exhibits spreading out to the left and right. The cousins and Brittany chose different directions, and I stood there with Ryan, staring up at a large cable hanging from the ceiling.

"Whoa? What is this?" I moved closer to a circular barrier that had been set up in the middle of the entrance. I stepped up on the concrete step and peered over at a circle of pegs that stood at the edge of the closed-in area.

Ryan stepped up next to me.

"This is a Foucault Pendulum. It demonstrates the earth's rotation."

I stared down as the ball attached to the bottom of the

cable swung back and forth, back and forth. Then it pushed over one of the pegs.

Ryan jumped, which made me jump.

"Did you see that? The earth is moving!"

I laughed. "It looks like a fancy-pants bowling game."

Ryan hit his forehead with his fist. "But it's *so* much more."

I walked around the circle, so I could examine the contraption from other angles.

Ryan followed. "It's a miracle, Allie. Think about it! When did you first learn that the earth rotates?"

"I dunno. Maybe third grade?"

"And how many times a day do you think about the fact that the earth is rotating?"

I raised one eyebrow. "Like, none."

Ryan put his face near mine. "But it's happening. And this pendulum shows it. As the earth moves, the pegs move. And eventually—bam—the pendulum knocks them over, one by one."

"Who's the poor person who has to pick those pegs up?" I asked.

"Who cares about that when supernatural things are happening around us all the time! And we're so wrapped up in the little details that we never take the time to think about it."

I watched as people in the crowd stepped up to look over at the exhibit. I raised my eyes up and followed the cable of the pendulum all the way to where it was attached to the dome.

"What do you mean by supernatural?" I asked.

"It's not something a human can invent or control. It's designed by the God of the Universe." Ryan was quiet for a minute. Then he put his hand on my shoulder. "And that causes me to think, if God is doing this super huge thing—making the earth turn—and I don't even realize it, then what other little miracles is he working in my life right now, that I'm also

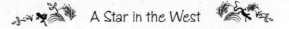

missing? I'm telling you, Allie, He's at work. We just gotta take the time to notice."

As Ryan wrapped up, another peg fell.

Hunter called from the left hallway. "Ryan! Come check out this moon exhibit!"

Ryan looked over at me. "You wanna come, squirt? And consider some more miracles? See why I love science so much?"

I shook my head. "Nah. I think I want to ponder this one right now."

"Okay, that's cool. I'll be with Hunter just down that hall. Don't forget the life-sized periodic table." Ryan spread his arms out from side to side. "Call me when you get to it. I don't want you to see it without me."

I nodded. "You're scaring me a little with that enthusiasm."

Ryan shoved me a little on the step. "It's what big brothers are for."

He jumped off the step and headed toward waxing and waning moons or something like that. I stood frozen in place next to the pendulum. It was one of those moments when you know God is trying to talk to you, and you try real hard to listen, so the crowd noise drowns out around you and you feel like you're in some kind of dream.

The earth is turning. And you don't even notice.

"Allie?" a small hand tugged on my T-shirt, jolting me out of my daydream.

I looked down, and there was Angela—the girl from the Doowylloh sign.

I smiled. "Hey, hiking buddy! How's the knee?"

Angela reached down and rubbed it. She still had the Ariel Band-Aid attached. "It's getting better. Can you help me?"

I looked around to see if I could spot Angela's dad, but I

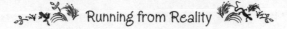

didn't know if I would recognize him after seeing him just once on the trail and in sunglasses.

"Sure, I can," I said. "I helped with the bloody knee, didn't I? Whatcha got for me today?"

"I can't find my daddy. I had lots of energy, so we hiked up here to see the planets, and now I'm a little lost."

"Hmmm. When did you last see him?"

She shrugged and shook her head. "I don't know. Maybe an hour."

I stared down at her cute face with the dirt smudges on her chin and thought about how frantic my parents would be if I was lost.

Angela pointed to the front doors of the Observatory. "I should go back to the car. I know my momma's there."

"Is your car in the Observatory parking lot?"

Angela shook her head again. "It's down the hiking trail. Not very far though. Can you take me? Please?"

I nodded. "O . . . kay."

I thought a minute, about whether I should call Ryan, Brittany, a security guard . . .

"You're the person I need," Angela said.

And I have everything I need.

"Let's go." I grabbed Angela's hand to help her off the step.

"Wait, I gotta bring this suitcase." With her other hand, Angela reached for the handle on a rolling, carry-on size pink and purple suitcase. Goosebumps raised on my arms when I noticed it had a sequined-silver star in the middle of it.

CHAPTER 23

Map Magic

M y momma's not feeling very good," Angela said, as we exited the tall, double doors at the entrance to the Observatory. "We need to get to my grandma's so she can have my brother."

"Where's that?" I asked.

"Lompoc. It's a funny name for a town. We gotta go up a freeway and it's a little past Santa Barbara. We're moving in. She's sick, so we're gonna help her."

"Oh."

"We used to live in Santa Ana, but my daddy lost his job and now we gotta leave that house."

"Oh."

"Our tire is shredded, and we don't have any more money to fix it. Well, except the gas money, but we gotta save that."

I gulped.

"But it's okay, 'cause we have lots of snacks to eat until God sends the miracle."

"A tire?"

"Yeah. That's easy for God, but I hope he hurries cause the car is getting cold at night."

"You've been sleeping in your car?"

Angela put her finger to her lips.

"Don't tell anyone. I think it's against the law."

"Oh."

We came to the end of the lawn in front of the Observatory, and I pointed down the hill to the parking lot.

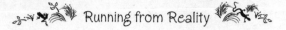
"Are you sure your family isn't down there?"

Angela nodded. "Yeah. We came from that trail."

She pointed to a dirt trail that veered off to the left.

"I don't know this trail at all, Angela." My temples throbbed and my heart raced.

"But I know you're supposed to help," she said.

I watched as families ventured off on the trail with their little kids and strollers. It looked harmless enough. "Let's sit here a minute," I said, and Angela and I piled onto the grass. "I have a map that we can look at."

Angela's eyes brightened. "I like maps."

I unzipped my backpack, reached into the crumpled lunch bag, and pulled out the map. My hand bumped the burner phone that hung in a top pocket.

"Aw, wait. I need to text someone first."

I handed the map to Angela, who opened it all the way up, spread it out on the grass, and lay on her tummy to look at it.

I typed out a text message to Ryan.

> Helping a lost little girl. Will meet you at life-
> sized periodic table in thirty minutes.

I hit send. I figured that would be plenty of time to run down the trail, find the car, and send this family on their way to the birth of their baby.

I was wrong.

"Angela, how long did it take for you and your dad to get to the Observatory?" I huffed and puffed as we climbed up and then scrambled down some steep parts on the dirt trail. I looked back and was relieved that I could still see the domes.

"I didn't pay attention. Sometimes I ran." Angela put her hand on her stomach. "I'm getting hungry."

"Is your car parked in a lot with other cars, or is it on a road that has houses?"

"Houses," Angela said. "Big, pretty ones." She stretched her one hand out to the side, keeping the other on the handle to that suitcase, which was kicking up dust as she rolled it behind us.

"I like your suitcase," I said. "I saw one like it the other day on the plane."

"It's new," Angela said. "A guy just gave it to me."

I stopped. "A guy? Like, a man? At the Observatory?"

No way.

Angela nodded. "I was crying on the grass, because I couldn't find my daddy. Then a guy came up and said, 'Here, this is for you.'"

"And he just left the suitcase with you? Angela, you should never take . . ."

"He said 'It has everything you need.' And that made me stop crying."

Double no way.

"What was the guy's name?"

"I forgot to ask. But he said he came from a place called Joy . . . Z. Something like that."

"New Jersey?"

Angela shook her head. "That's not what it sounded like, but maybe."

I stared down into Angela's hope-filled eyes.

The earth is turning and you don't even notice.

Angela started walking again, and I didn't say anything for a while. I looked down at my watch. We'd been on the trail for ten minutes. I needed to make a decision, since I wasn't going to make it back in time to meet my brother at the periodic table.

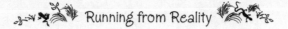

"Hang on, Angela. I need to send another text." I stopped, pulled my backpack off my back, and reached for the burner phone.

It's taking a little longer. I'll keep you posted.

A text came back right away from Ryan:

Where are you, Allie?

Oh no.

Walking a little girl to her car. I have a map.
Don't worry.

Ryan was quick to respond again and he sounded worried.

Allie! I'm coming to find you.

No, Ryan. I'll be right back.

I don't want you getting lost!

That comment frustrated me just a tiny bit.

I'm not Ruby. I'll be fine.

I could almost hear my brother sigh.

Allie!

I took a deep breath and blew it out. I looked up at Angela, reached over, and put my hand on her shoulder.

"Let's go find your parents."

I grabbed the handle of the suitcase to take a turn pulling it through the dirt. Up ahead, I spotted a sign.

"Oh, look! I think this will tell us exactly where to go."

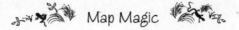

Angela perked up a bit.

"I saw this sign before. Yep, there's the rock that looks like a heart."

Sure enough, a rock that was shaped like a heart sat at the base of the sign.

"Okay, then, let's see what the sign says." I pointed my finger at the top line. "Hollywood Sign, four miles. I think we can skip that one today, what do you think?" I tapped my index finger on my cheek.

"Yeah. Skip," Angela said. "We went there already."

I continued with the next option. "Mount Hollywood. That seems like it goes up."

"I know we have to go down," Angela added.

The next line showed a street name. "Sandy Beach Trailhead. Does that sound familiar? Sandy Beach?"

Her eyes opened wide and she smiled big. "Yes! Sandy Beach! I was expecting a real beach to be there, but no."

"Okay," I checked my watch. "We're really close, only .2 miles. We can do this! Do you want to run a little?"

"Yes! We can get to the snacks quicker."

So, we jogged. It was easy, because it was downhill—but that made me a little nervous for what I would have to do on the way back. We passed some families coming up the trail, so when that happened, we slowed a bit so our suitcase wouldn't cover them in dust.

"This is fun," Angela said. "I'm glad we're friends, Allie."

"Me too."

We finally rounded the last turn, and I could see the trailhead where it led out into a neighborhood of homes built into the hills—just like the ones on Star Drive.

"This is it!" Angela jumped up and down and pointed across the street. "I remember that red house."

"Okay, then, which way is your car? To the right or to the left?"

Just as I said that, I spotted a young man walking down the middle of the street. He had a black athletic bag slung across his shoulder, and a phone to his ear. Something didn't seem right, so I grabbed Angela by the elbow and pulled her down behind a parked truck. I put my finger up to my lips.

"Shhh. Be real quiet till he passes us."

Angela looked at me with wide eyes and nodded.

We scrunched way down on the same level with the truck tires.

I could hear the boy's conversation as he passed.

"Yeah, I'm going back to 51415 at 7:00. Have the car on the curb by 7:15. I can't wait to dim those lights for good."

My mouth went dry, and I had to steady myself on the side of the truck.

"Is everything okay?" Angela whispered so quietly I could barely hear her.

I nodded and put my finger to my lips again. I watched as the young man passed the truck, and then began running down the street at a frantic pace.

Looking to dim some lights? Well, buddy, you've got another thing coming if you try to mess with the Carroways.

"Can we get up now?" Angela was folded into a compact little ball between the curb and the truck.

I watched a moment or so more to make sure the Hollywoodlum was long gone.

I reached out my hand to lift Angela back up.

"Coast is clear." I brushed off my pants. "Now, can you remember which way we go to get to your car?"

Angela smiled. "Oh, yeah. It's easy now. Just over there by that brown house with the pointy roof. Our car is by the round street sign that says "City of LA." Angela broke into a run, and

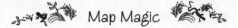

I followed a few feet until she came to an older model, green minivan, that had the passenger-side door open.

Angela put both her arms out. "Momma! Are you feeling better?"

The slightly built, but super pregnant dark-haired woman stepped down out of the van. And right then, Angela's dad came jogging up behind us and grabbed Angela up in his arms.

"Angela! Where have you been? I told you to stay in the planet room." Angela's dad squeezed her in a tight hug, kissed her head, and finally put her down.

"It was too dark in there and I couldn't find you, but I found my friend, Allie. And I got a suitcase with everything we need—I think. That's what the Joy-Zee guy said anyway."

The woman looked over the suitcase. "Joy-Zee?" Then she held out her hand to shake mine. "Hi, I'm Jenny, and this is my husband, David. I'm afraid we're a little down on our luck."

"It's nice to meet you. Congratulations on the baby."

Jenny rubbed her belly. "Thank you. I just hope I don't have him right here on this road."

I looked down at the back tire of the van. Angela was right. Shredded.

Angela's dad hung his head. "This is what we get for sight-seeing when we should have been driving straight through to my mom's house. I knew these tires didn't have much left in them."

"Maybe there's a tire in here!" Angela grabbed the handle to the suitcase and tilted it back so she could lay it on the street next to the van. "Oh, no." She frowned. "There's a lock on it."

"A lock?" I said. "What kind of lock?" I walked over and inspected the little metal padlock that had pink plastic molded around the corners.

Hmmmmm.

I pulled my backpack off my back and unzipped it. My hand

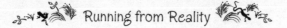

shook as I felt for the now very familiar Bag of Wonders. Could that silly key fit a diary *and* a suitcase lock?

I pulled out the key, and remembered Ryan's words from just a little while ago:

If God is doing this super huge thing—making the earth turn—and I don't even realize it, then what other little miracles is he working in my life right now, that I'm also missing? I'm telling you Allie, he's at work. We just gotta take the time to notice."

I held it up. "I have a key, and the pink plastic matches. It's worth a try. My cousin Kendall says these keys fit all kinds of things."

I knelt next to the suitcase in the street. My hand still shook as I tried to match the end of the key with the opening on the little padlock. This was a long shot, and I sure didn't want to disappoint Angela.

I jiggled the key—using Kendall's special technique. It moved back and forth, and clicked a little, but nothing.

"Turn it the other way," Angela said.

That didn't make sense, but then this whole trip didn't make sense.

So, I turned it the other way.

And the padlock popped open!

CHAPTER 24

Everything You Need

It was just like Christmas morning. *Except* it was three days before Thanksgiving, and I was out in the middle of the street in a strange neighborhood in Hollywood. There *was* a pregnant couple, but they were traveling in a van, not on a donkey, and I'm pretty sure they weren't planning to name their little baby boy Jesus.

Angela squealed and jumped up and down as she pulled some wrapped presents out of the suitcase. Her parents stood there, jaws dropping open, as she unwrapped each one.

"My own baby doll—now we both can rock a baby together!" she said to her mom.

The next present was some crayons and coloring books. "I love to color," Angela said.

Of course, you do.

The next present was obviously for the baby—a package of newborn diapers.

And there was a gift bag full of snacks—candy, nuts, granola bars, and some packages of dried fruit.

"This is incredible," David said. "This can't all be for us, can it?"

"Hey," I shrugged. "Never argue with a guy from Joy-Zee. And I had the key."

There were a few more presents. Some bath products, a burner phone, and a Bible.

Jenny couldn't hold back the tears. "Our phone has been broken for days."

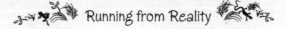

David picked up the Bible and flipped through its pages. An envelope fell out that had something written on the outside. David read it out loud to all of us.

"And my God will meet all your needs according to the riches of his glory in Christ Jesus. Philippians 4:19"

David carefully loosened the glue on the envelope, and had to stop for a minute to wipe his eyes when he looked inside. He reached in and pulled out money. Three-hundred dollars worth of money.

Jenny started to sob.

Angela moved over and hugged her mom.

"Are you okay, Mommy?"

Jenny nodded and wiped rivers of tears on her sleeve. "Yes, honey. I'm fine. These are happy tears."

"Oh, good. Did God do the miracle?"

"Yeah, he did. And he did it with the help of your friend here . . ." Jenny turned to me.

"I'm sorry, I'm so flustered. What is your name again?"

It took me a minute to clear the lump in my throat, but when I did, I spoke up, loud and clear. I didn't care who heard.

"My name is Allie. Allie Carroway. You might have heard about my family. We're on a TV show called *Carried Away with the Carroways*."

CHAPTER 25

Busting the Enemy

I spent a few more minutes with Angela's family, but then I took off back toward the trailhead. The Hollywoodlum was after the Gabi-girls' house and that was just not acceptable.

I wonder how far I am from Star *Drive?*

I sat down on the curb and pulled out my map of the Hollywood Hills. I had to spread it out on the street in front of me, look up Sandy Beach Trailhead, and then find Star Drive.

It was only about four blocks away.

I figured I had two choices. Go back to the Observatory—a half mile or so uphill, or take off toward the house. But what if the Hollywoodlum was going that way already? Did I want to face him myself?

Or I could call in reinforcements. After all, we had a plan.

I pulled out the burner phone and sent a group text to my team:

> Operation "Shine your light" is under way. Get
> yourselves home asap. I'll meet you there.

Then I called Ryan.

"Hello? Allie? Where are you? I'm out here in the parking lot of the Observatory. Did you come down here?"

"Ryan, listen carefully! We don't have time. I'm at the Sandy Beach Trailhead, and I'm on my way to the Gabi-girls' house. I spotted the Hollywoodlum, and I overheard him say he was going to 51415 Star Drive tonight at seven o'clock."

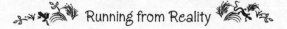

I gathered up the map, slung my backpack over my shoulder, and began to jog while holding the phone to my ear.

"Allie, stay away from that house. I'll call the police, and we'll get down there to pick you up as soon as we can."

I had to stop a minute to catch my breath.

"Allie! Are you still there?! Don't go near the house!"

My brother had never sounded frantic a minute in his life until now.

"Okay. I'll hide somewhere nearby and I'll flag you down when I see the van."

Ryan sighed. "I'm not happy with that either, but I guess I have no choice. Why didn't you just meet me at the periodic table?"

"I'm sorry. It's just—God was at work, and this time I noticed."

"Huh?"

"Just like the earth is turning. It's your fault for teaching me that."

"You're blaming me for this?"

"I'll tell you the story later. I gotta go." I pushed the end button on the phone and then checked for any returned texts from my cousins. Nope. I stopped to take a minute to refold the map so that my route was visible on the front. Then I tightened up the straps of my backpack and broke into an all-out run up and down the narrow streets of the Hollywood Hills.

When I arrived on Star Drive, I slowed. I don't think my heart could pump any faster than it was right then. Every nerve was on high alert as I creeped along the side of the road, ducking in and around mailboxes, trashcans, and bushes. I saw no one, and only two cars drove by. I looked both ways, then jetted across the street from the Gabi-girls house—51417 Star Drive. I flew up the steps to the third balcony and took a seat on a metal bistro chair, at the perfect height to duck my head behind the concrete wall, but then peek over whenever I heard a noise.

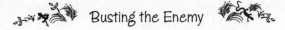

Looks like this place is empty. I wonder what movie star lived here?

The place was so quiet it was eerie. Not even a barking dog, and only a car or two drove by. Some hikers walked by about twenty minutes into my surveillance, but they didn't stop in at any of the houses on the street that I could see. A police car drove by next, and it slowed in front of the Gabi-girls' house but then vanished.

Finally, about forty-five minutes later, the red van came down the street. I could see Ryan's head turning left and right, scouring the streets for the little sister who's neck he would wring as soon as he could find her.

I stood and waved both my hands in the air from the third story balcony, and Brittany saw me. She pointed, and Ryan stopped.

He rolled down his window.

"Allie Kate Carroway, get down here."

"Hurry, Allie!" Brittany waved me down, and I creeped down the stairway, keeping watch both ways on the street. Someone slid the side door to the van open, and I jumped in.

"Allie, are you okay?" Lola put her hand to her mouth. "How did you get here?"

"I walked," I said. "I had a map."

I smiled at Kendall, who could only cross her arms and shake her head.

"Is the Hollywoodlum really coming tonight?" Hunter leaned forward in his swivel chair.

"That's what I overheard him say on the phone when he ran by me."

"Wow," Ruby said. "We gotta stop him."

"That's right," Kendall said.

"NO, that's not right!" Ryan craned his neck around to look at us. "The police will be here, and they'll catch him."

"Oh, yes, what was I thinking?" I turned my head toward the cousins, put my hand up to the side of my face to block my mouth, and whispered, "But we're gonna slow him down first."

Ryan pulled the van into the garage and we all ran up to the front door.

"Turn on every light you see," Brittany said. "If he thinks someone is here, then he'll go away."

"No," Ryan said. "Don't turn any lights on at all. We *want* him to come up to the house, and get started with the vandalism so the police can catch him in the act. I want you all in your rooms. We'll grab some food and you can go eat up there. Don't come down till I tell you the coast is clear."

I piled so many snacks on a tray that it was a little heavy to carry.

"Put it on the dumbwaiter, darling," Kendall said in her British accent.

And so I did. I pulled the rope, and then we raced up the stairs to see who could get to the food first.

It was me.

Ryan and Brittany stayed downstairs to wait for the police, and the cousins all came into Kendall's and my room.

"Okay," Hunter said. "We've got the water balloons all spread out on the balcony. As soon as we finish eating, I say we take our positions and wait."

I looked at my watch. "He said around 7:00, so we have a little time to kill."

"What should we do?" Ruby said.

"I think you should let me tell you all about what was in that bag I got at the airport."

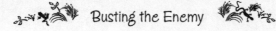

"Yes, tell us!" Ruby's eyes sparkled as she sat down on the rug in front of the wingback chairs. Lola and Hunter sat down next to her, and Kendall took the other chair. They were mesmerized as I told them about the Band-Aids, the map, the brochure, and the headlamp with the matching address and scripture about shining the light of Jesus. I shared about the key, and how it somehow opened Gabi's diary that I found in the dumbwaiter *and* the sequined-star suitcase of a little girl whose family really needed what was inside. I felt like I was telling a made-up, exaggerated Carroway fable.

But every bit of it was reality.

"It's 6:55. We better get to our stations." Hunter was even more focused on saving the Gabi-girls' house now that he knew the story about the diary. "We need to be real quiet out on the balcony, though. And no lights until I give the signal."

We crossed the hallway to the room where Hunter had been staying. His slider door led out to a balcony that faced the front of the house, and just happened to be right over the entryway to the house, one story down. Thankfully, the walls were concrete, so no one would be able to see our bodies, and we could peek over as soon as we heard a sound.

We waited, and waited, and while I waited, I thought about Matthew 5:14–15:

You are the light of the world. A city on a hilltop that cannot be hidden.

This whole trip, I had been trying to hide. But it never worked, not for one single moment. People kept finding me, and though they didn't recognize me as Allie Carroway—they sure noticed something.

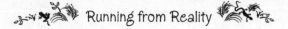

Laying there in the dark on the balcony, I finally realized what it was. It was Jesus, shining through me.

"Let your light shine before men so they will see your good deeds and praise your Father in Heaven."

Well, I sure wanted that. Maybe it was time to look at my life in a whole new way.

"Hey," Hunter whispered. "Someone's down there."

Hunter still had his cowboy hat on, but it was black so it didn't show up in the dark. He peeked over the wall and then scrunched back down.

"Yep, that's him alright. He just went under the street light. He's got a black athletic bag slung over his shoulder."

My heart started pumping harder. I poked my head up over the wall.

"There's a car way down there that doesn't have its lights on. It's moving forward, then stopping, then moving forward . . ."

"Maybe he brought a team of hoodlums," Lola put her hands to her cheeks and breathed out hard.

I squinted and sighed when the car came closer into view.

"It's the police."

"Oh, good." Ruby peeked over the wall. "Let's go back inside."

Kendall held her hand out. "No. Let's do this . . . for the Gabi-girls."

"He's coming closer," Hunter said. "When he gets up to the door, I'll count to three, and then we bust the enemy."

"I'm scared," Lola said.

"Use the fear to throw harder," I said. "Send him a message that you don't mess with bayou kids."

"Yeah," Ruby said.

We each grabbed a water balloon with both hands and sat in a crouched position. We heard nothing for a minute, but then

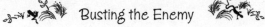

there were footsteps, and zipping. Wood knocking together. Then a simple sentence:

"Okay, lights—I'm snuffing you out."

And then Hunter counted.

"Three . . . two . . . one!"

We all stood at once, and chucked the balloons at the young man down below as he tried to swing a bat. After we threw those, we loaded up again. And again. And again.

You know how sometimes water balloons don't break, so it just feels like you've been hit by a round brick? Yeah. That's probably how the Hollywoodlum felt at that moment, cause none of them broke. They bounced off his head, arms, shoulders, and then off the pavement.

"Ahhhhh! Hey!!! Stop!"

"Hit the lights!" Hunter yelled. And the Carroway cousins let our headlamps shine.

The Hollywoodlum lay on the ground, and—too bad for him—we didn't stop. We kept throwing water bricks until the two policemen from the car caught up to the house and ran to the door.

"Cease your attack!" One of them waved both arms back and forth in the air. "We got him!"

One more balloon dropped. Kendall's. And that one broke—right on the Hollywoodlum's head.

"Oops," Kendall said.

About that time, Ryan showed up, down below with another police officer.

"Where did these balloons come from?" the officer asked.

Ryan picked one up and looked up. He grinned.

"Looks like the Carroways got a little carried away—as usual." Then he pointed up at us. The police officers waved.

"Thanks, kids!" one of them said. "My family loves your show."

"Let me go!" the Hollywoodlum cried. "They attacked me! I didn't do anything!"

The officer turned the Hollywoodlum around and pulled his hands around to his back to cuff him.

"We've got you on camera, swinging a bat at this door. Let me guess, are you going to try to convince us that you live here and that you're locked out?"

The young man stayed quiet. "Would you believe that?"

The officer shook his head. "No, but you do have the right to remain silent . . ."

My cousins and I ran back into the house, and high-fived each other.

"That was awesome!" Lola yelled. "We busted a criminal and saved Hollywood!"

"And it was so fun!" Hunter whooped and hollered.

"Don't mess with the Carroways," I said. "Our lights will not be snuffed out."

"I can't wait to tell my parents," Lola said.

"Me too!" Ruby added

"And Allie, you have to tell everyone about your bag of wonders," Lola smiled.

"Think of all the stories we can share at Thanksgiving." Kendall flipped her red hair around. "This trip has been the best!"

I crossed my arms in front of me and looked around at all my cousins, and shook my head.

"Umm . . . are you forgetting something? We can't tell anyone *anything*. We have a deal. Everything that's happened is just between us. Forever."

Kendall shook her head and stomped her foot. "What? That's not fair! When we made that deal we had no idea we'd

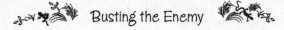

be running into miracles! Everyone needs to know! I think we should be able to tell about this on the show."

"Show?" I said. "You mean the show we're on strike from?"

"Well, that was your idea," Kendall said.

"So, you're blaming *me*?" I sat down on the recliner in Hunter's room. "People—you were complaining that you were overwhelmed with the show and duck-hunting season, and raking leaves too. And you were tired of having everyone know about your lives. Remember?"

Hunter looked down at the ground. "I guess we have been doing a lot of complaining. All that stuff doesn't sound like such a big deal now."

"I guess if Gabi could do the show business thing, we can too." Kendall shoved me over and joined me on the recliner.

"And we do have each other," Lola added.

"Okay," I said, and I stood and put my hand out. "Let's make a deal. We stop running from reality, and instead, we let our lights shine out through the lives God has given us."

"I like it," Ruby said. "I don't like trying to be someone else. I miss wearing my jeans."

"And I guess maybe I do look a *little* like a poinsettia with this hair." Kendall grinned.

"And the ocean really isn't turquoise." Lola ran her fingers through her streak.

"Can I keep my cowboy hat? Please?" Hunter grabbed the brim with both hands and tugged it down on his head, which made his ears bend over.

We laughed.

"Of course," Lola said. "It's definitely you. But we still gotta do something about those shorts!"

CHAPTER 26

Reality Check

I had a new sense of purpose on my return home. My goal was to embrace everything and anything that God brought my way— from here on out. As I walked my neighborhood Thanksgiving morning, I said a prayer for each house as I passed it, and I asked that God would show me how to shine my light. I also remembered little Emmy—from the ER.

Lord, help her to stop running. Just like you helped me to stop running.

Joy filled my heart as I passed by the Lickety Split construction site. While we were away, walls had gone up, and I breathed in deep and smelled the aroma of freshly sawed wood.

I can't wait to see what adventures we'll cook up in there.

I felt so good to be home that I did a few back flips, and then jogged back toward our house to see if Mom needed some help preparing Thanksgiving dinner. As I rounded the corner toward our driveway, I saw a strange car backing out of our driveway.

It stopped, and a man and two kids got out. A boy and a girl who both looked my age.

"Hello," the red-haired man said. "You must be Allie. I'm Andrew Doonsberry, and these are my kids, Parker and Madison."

A little joy leaked out of me at that moment. These were the new owners of my house. Well, in a few days.

I tried to grin, and held out my hand.

"Nice to meet you, sir. Welcome to the neighborhood."

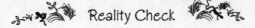

I glanced over at the kids. Parker smiled. Madison backed away and glared.

Uh-oh.

"We were just taking some measurements for furniture," Mr. Doonsberry said. "Your parents were very gracious to let us come and do that on Thanksgiving."

"Your room is too small for all my stuff," Madison said. "Plus, it's painted a baby color. I'll be changing it immediately—if I even decide to use that room."

"Madi, be nice!" Mr. Doonsberry shook his head. "I'm afraid my daughter is a little frustrated about the move."

I nodded. "I understand."

And I really did.

Madi just rolled her eyes at me.

"Well, we better get on our way. I've got some work to do at the hotel, and I promised the kids we'd find the best restaurant in town, so I can treat them to some Louisiana food for Thanksgiving."

He seemed like such a nice guy. Handsome and sweet. His son too.

"It was nice to meet you, Allie," Parker said, and he walked back to his car and jumped in. Mr. Doonsberry did the same.

Madi lingered. Crossed her arms in front of her. Glared at me, and said, "You're nothin' special."

Then she turned, got in the car, and they drove away.

CHAPTER 27

God of Wonders

The day we filmed the Carroway Family Easter episode—Friday, February 14th—was the day my heart was changed forever.

The whole scene was weird. Pastel-colored placemats lined the dinner table filled with fake lily centerpieces at my Aunt Kassie and Uncle Wayne's house. My whole family sat around three separate tables with platters and bowls filled with deviled eggs, scalloped potatoes, and baked beans. A little marshmallow bunny sat in the middle of each of our heavy-duty, segmented paper plates. Camo-printed plastic eggs were hidden all over inside the house—because it was raining—so that after dinner the little kids could have their "Easter" egg hunt.

My cousins and I exchanged Valentines as we waited for the film crew to get set up.

Hunter opened mine. It had a picture of a dinosaur, and it said, "No bones about it—you're great, Valentine!"

"Ha! A paleontologist pun! I love it!"

"Here you go, roomie." Kendall gave me a Valentine. It was a homemade coupon book. The first one said, "Good for hanging up one strand of twinkle lights."

"Really? You're finally gonna let me hang them?"

Kendall shrugged. "Why not? They might inspire me to write songs about hope and light."

I smiled.

Ruby and Lola sat across the table reading their cards.

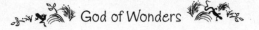

Ruby handed me a conversation heart that said, "Hey, Cuz!" I popped it in my mouth, but then panicked and spit it out.

"Was this manufactured in a plant that processes peanuts?"

Lola looked at the package. "Nah, I think you're good. They only manufacture sugar."

Mamaw came out of the kitchen carrying a platter of ham that the new caterers had prepared.

"I just want y'all to know, this is a BAD HAM. I don't recommend you put one single piece in your mouth."

"What?" My mom picked up a piece. "How can someone ruin a ham?" She lifted the morsel to her mouth, tried to bite into it, and grabbed a mason jar of water and gulped it down. "How do you even make a ham this salty?"

"It must have been one tough pig," Mamaw added. "I almost needed Papaw's chainsaw to get it off the bone. It's a good thing I'm cooking our *real* Easter dinner."

Our director, Zeke, began barking instructions. "Okay, Carroways, you know the drill. When I yell, 'action,'" Ray is gonna pray, and then you'll all dig in. The ham does look scary, so eat at your own risk. Action!"

Papaw stood. "Please bow with me. Heavenly Father, we thank you for the day you rose from the grave to give eternal life to all those who believe in you. We are grateful for the lives you have given us, and we even thank you for the ability to share our lives, as imperfect as they may be, with people who watch our show. Watch over them, Father, give them hope, and bless their families, just as you have blessed us every day of our lives. Thank you for being at work when we don't even notice. In Jesus' name, amen."

We all started eating—but not the ham. It was the consistency of bark, and could have been used as roof tiles for the Lickety Split—which was due to be finished in the next couple of weeks.

"Hey, squirt, I got something for you." Ryan and Brittany had flown in for our "Easter" celebration, and to go through the storage shed to clean out some things we had moved out of our house in November.

Ryan handed me an envelope.

"What's in here?" I asked. "A valentine?"

Ryan grinned. "Dude, you'll have to open it and find out."

At the next filming break, I asked Hannah if I could go to my room for a minute.

"Yeah, but be back in five minutes. We're bringing in a new ham and you don't want to miss it."

I excused myself, and ran upstairs to Kendall's room. I liked it here, but I really missed my too-small-room with the baby-colored walls. I couldn't understand why Madison didn't like the color. Blue is soothing, which sounds like something she could have used.

I plopped down on my stomach on the bed, and peeled the sealed envelope open. I pulled out a letter—a real, handwritten letter! The writing wasn't too neat, but the words popped out clearly and soaked into my heart and soul:

Dear Allie,

I'm the kid who gave you a bag at the Dallas-Fort Worth Airport. Remember me? I bought a lot of food and you helped me pay for it.

Anyway, I feel like a doofus. Our youth group was on a mission trip, and before we left, we each put together a "blessing bag." We prayed about what to put in it, and then we prayed about who to give it to. Well, as you know, you got mine.

But, dude, I gotta apologize, because I gave you

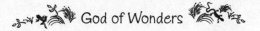

the wrong bag! That's what I get for being in such a hurry, and for using the same brown bags for everything. I meant to give you a bag with some trail mix, mints, and a little Bible promise book. Instead, you got some worthless junk that I think has been in my backpack for a couple of years since I lived in my grandma's house.

Will you forgive me?

Sincerely,
Nathan Fremont

P.S. I thought you looked familiar, but didn't realize who you were till I got home and watched TV.

P.S.S. Also, your brother is my 8th grade science teacher. Isn't that crazy? If you're ever in Santa Barbara, look me up and we'll switch bags.

I read the letter I think eight times. Each time it jolted me. *Trail mix? With nuts? Seriously? That bag would have killed me!* I flipped over on my back, stared up at the ceiling, and prayed.

Thank you, Lord, for being a God of wonders. I know I'll never truly understand everything you are doing all the time, but I'm here, and I'm yours. Use me any way you want to shine your light in the world. Amen.

I lay there, still as could be. And at that moment, I'm sure I felt the earth turn.

faithgirlz

Princess in Camo
Missy and Mia Robertson
with Jill Osborne

Allie's Bayou Rescue (Book 1)

Life hasn't been easy lately for twelve-year-old Allie Carroway. Not only does she have to be careful about what she eats and keep her asthma treatment with her at all times, but rumor has it that if she has one more serious asthma attack, her family may move to Arizona—far away from the Louisiana Bayou and the extended family that she loves and stars with in the reality TV show, Carried Away with the Carroways.

And now would be a terrible time to go. Uncle Wayne and Aunt Kassie are about to adopt twelve-year-old Hunter—the first boy to join the Carroway family in a long time. Allie and her cousins—Kendall, Ruby, and Lola—have never allowed a boy to set foot in their treehouse meeting place, the "Diva Duck Blind." And if Allie's cousins have any say, they'll keep it that way. But Allie can't ignore that still, small voice inside her, telling her things must change if Hunter is to be honored and accepted into the family.

The cousins devise an initiation for Hunter at Mamaw and Papaw's house with four challenges—Louisiana bayou style—including frogs, hunting, and a scary shed rumored to be the place where a mysterious long lost uncle disappeared. A blackout on the bayou the night of the initiation heightens the stakes when Hunter goes missing, and Allie and the girls must face unfamiliar obstacles to bring the family back together.

This series explores the nature of a family filled with social, cultural, and physical diversity. In a world splashed with class and camouflage, the cousins are constantly looking for ways to love unconditionally through all the hiccups, with the love and faith of family.

Available in stores and online!

ZONDERkidz™

faithgirlz

Princess in Camo

Missy and Mia Robertson
with Jill Osborne

Dog Show Disaster (Book 3)

In the third book in the Princess in Camo series—*Dog Show Disaster*—just maybe, reality TV star Allie Carroway is in over her head! When Allie is unanimously elected by her schoolmates as the Student Project Manager of this year's end-of-the-year school carnival and fundraiser she is excited. Her friends and family love her idea of having a dog show as part of the festivities and know it will be the perfect way to raise money for the local animal shelter.

But almost immediately things start going haywire. Big and small disasters start to happen, one after the other, and soon Allie cannot imagine how the Ouachita Middle School Bark Fest can possibly be a success. But with the super support of the Carroway cousins, family, and friends, and a strong faith and trust that God knows exactly what is needed and when, things start to turn around; but not without a few hurdles, including a bit of bullying and rivalries, along the way!

This third book in the Faithgirlz Princess in Camo series is the perfect addition to this unique storyline about a fun and faith-filled family in a world of class and camouflage.

Available in stores and online!

faithgirlz

Princess in Camo

Missy and Mia Robertson
with Jill Osborne

Finding Cabin Six (Book 4)

From authors Missy and Mia Robertson comes the fourth book in the Princess in Camo series—*Finding Cabin Six*. It's summertime—and when you're a Carroway, that means heading to camp for an exciting week of fun, friends, and faith-building. But this summer will be different—rumor has it that the camp is struggling and may be sold to a resort developer at the end of the season. Cousins Allie, Kendall, Lola, Ruby, and Hunter are devastated by the news, so they set out on a mission to save the camp!

It's a job that will take some strong prayer, a clever plan, and a little sleuthing, made difficult by the constant presence of Allie's new "friend," Madison Doonsberry, and California surfer-boy Nathan Fremont. But when they uncover information about a similar camp struggle in the past and discover clues that lead them to the true story behind the disappearance of legendary girls' cabin six, the cousins realize that they're right in the middle of God's plan to grow them closer together and teach them the value of lost people.

This fourth book in the Faithgirlz Princess in Camo series is the perfect addition to this unique storyline about a fun and faith-filled family in a world of class and camouflage.

Available in stores and online!

Connect with Faithgirlz!

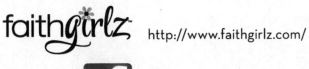 http://www.faithgirlz.com/

 www.facebook.com/Faithgirlz/

www.instagram.com/zonderkidz_faithgirlz/

CPSIA information can be obtained
at www.ICGtesting.com
Printed in the USA
LVOW08s0024140318
569609LV00005BA/121/P